THE

When Sister Kaye Harcourt finds herself roped into a fascinating new project to help children of restricted growth she's delighted. But not so pleased when old flame Dr Orson Latimer joins the team—for how can the happy ward live up to its reputation with *him* around?

Books you will enjoy
in our Doctor Nurse series:

RING FOR A NURSE by Lisa Cooper
DOCTOR IN THE ANDES by Dana James
DR ARROGANT, MD by Lindsay Hicks
BELOVED ANGEL by Lucinda Oakley
NURSE WESTON'S NEW JOB by Clare Lavenham
CANDLES FOR THE SURGEON by Helen Upshall
THE RELUCTANT ANGEL by Sarah Franklin
NURSE ON NEURO by Ann Jennings
THORN-TREE MIDWIFE by Barbara Perkins
NO DOCTORS, PLEASE by Lydia Balmain
A DEDICATED NURSE by Jean Evans
HEART OF A SURGEON by Alexina Rawdon
SISTER IN A SARONG by Jenny Ashe
SIGH FOR A SURGEON by Lynne Collins
A TIME TO HEAL by Sarah Franklin
NURSE IN WAITING by Janet Ferguson
HEART MURMURS by Grace Read
SNOW SISTER by Kate Ashton
DOCTOR KNOWS BEST by Ann Jennings
CINDERELLA SRN by Anna Ramsay
JONATHAN PAGET, MD by Elizabeth Petty
THE SURGEON AT ST PETER'S by Rhona Trezise
MARRYING A DOCTOR by Elizabeth Harrison

THE HAPPY WARD

BY

LISA COOPER

MILLS & BOON LIMITED
15–16 BROOK'S MEWS
LONDON W1A 1DR

First published in Great Britain 1985
by Mills & Boon Limited

© Lisa Cooper 1985

Australian copyright 1985
Philippine copyright 1985

ISBN 0 263 75019 1

Set in 11 on 11½ pt Linotron Times
03–0485–48,500

Photoset by Rowland Phototypesetting Ltd
Bury St Edmunds, Suffolk
Made and printed in Great Britain by
Richard Clay (The Chaucer Press) Ltd
Bungay, Suffolk

CHAPTER ONE

'I REMEMBER this.' Sister Kaye Harcourt picked up the heavy book with the often-mended cover. 'Everyone said it ought to have a new cover or we should have a new book, but it's still the same.'

'I was forgetting, Sister.' The small staff nurse eyed her with ill-concealed curiosity. 'You were here on the children's ward at some time.'

'It seemed ages ago when I decided to come back, but now, when I see things like the doctors' book and that chair in the duty room with the awful purple linen cover, it can't possibly be two years!'

'Why did you leave?' Nurse Grace Benson sensed that the new sister was approachable and could be rather good.

'I wanted to do midder,' said the new sister, putting the book sharply on the office desk. 'Well, perhaps you could tell me something about the patients, Nurse.'

She sat in the swivel chair facing her staff nurse and her huge dark eyes were sad. Her pale skin was smooth and added to the madonna calm of her lovely mouth, but the first smile had died and Nurse Benson knew that this was no time to pursue further confidences. 'I was told that the main ward is now in cubicles with the side wards kept for the children being investigated for PHS. Have we any in there now?'

'There are two expected tomorrow, Sister. The

5

little girl in side ward one is being transferred to the ward today and they want everything ready for the tests tomorrow at two o'clock.' Nurse Benson smiled. 'I'm very glad you've come, Sister. I know very little about Pituitary Hormone Syndrome and I was scared about tomorrow.'

'They will only measure them and make out charts and do various intelligence tests to get the general picture. The Path people will take blood and then when they are ready to make the test with Bovril, we take over and it all goes on from there.'

'You did say Bovril, Sister?'

'Yes, they discovered that if a child is given a certain amount of beef extract, the pituitary is stimulated to produce the growth hormone. If there is no change in the hormone level of the blood, then a part of the pituitary gland is not functioning and either has to be stimulated by injections of the hormone or a substitute given.'

'It sounds ridiculously simple.'

'Most really wonderful discoveries are, at least on the surface. But it isn't the end of the story by any means, I'm afraid. Some children have a separate condition that also restricts growth and they, poor little dears, can never be treated—not as far as we know with present medical knowledge. I suppose we must be thrilled that some can now be helped to grow to a normal height, but it does seem hard that not all can benefit from the treatment.'

'It sounds exciting. I didn't really want to come to this ward but I get more and more interested as fresh cases come in, and there isn't the noise and crying that I thought would go on day and night.'

'It was always a very happy ward, Nurse

Benson,' Sister Harcourt smiled. 'I'm sure it is the same now. I must confess that I missed it and the rest of Beatties.'

It was like slipping into a comfortable old dressing-gown. The wrought iron gates at the end of the driveway still hung vaguely askew and the flower beds surely had the same sculptured regiment of bedding plants that had been there when Senior Staff Nurse Harcourt had carried her cases down to the taxi two years ago, her eyes blinded by tears and her voice trembling when she told the driver to take her to Paddington Station. The colour of the wide entrance hall was different and she could no longer remember if it had been pale green or beige in the old days, but this ward was the same in spite of the cubicle curtains and the fresh-tiled floors in the side wards.

Even that book. Sister Harcourt tried not to think of the book. In it, she knew, she would find all the names of the doctors who had worked with children in the Princess Beatrice Hospital in South London. She knew that each name would have its list of likes and dislikes, idiosyncrasies and a brief description of what he or she had done that might be of interest to visitors. It was a tactful record that could be read before a doctor came to the ward, ensuring that Sister or Staff Nurse could mention matters relevant to the case they were seeing. A doctor who had been in the ward several years ago could be greeted by name and mention be made of his previous visit, a nicety that never failed to flatter and make for a good atmosphere.

'Would you like to see the child in the side ward first, Sister? She will be moving into the end cubicle as soon as the morning bed-baths are finished and the beds tidy.'

'Yes, I'll start there and you can fill me in as we go.' Kaye picked up the chart and frowned. 'Injuries to left arm and shoulder, abrasions and cuts on back and red patches on her legs. Any suggestions from the social services?'

She flicked over the sheets of paper under the clip on the board. 'Seen twice by Miss Brindle, the social worker, who believes the injuries were inflicted deliberately and not by accident as the parents say.'

They walked into the side ward, where a small girl sat up in bed wearing headphones and looking at a picture book. She glanced up and smiled and went back to her book.

'She seems very relaxed,' said Sister. 'How long has she been here?'

'Three days, Sister. Some of the bruises have faded already and the rash has almost gone.'

'What rash?'

'She has giant urticaria and has been coming to Out-patients for months. The strange thing is that it goes as soon as she comes in for treatment and is probably an allergy brought on by stress.' The nurse gave a short laugh. 'Allergic to the person who mistreats her, I would think.'

'We have no proof, have we? The best we can do is to treat the symptoms and alert the social worker in charge of her case. Meanwhile, make sure that she plays with some of the other children and see how she reacts to them.'

'She doesn't like playing with them. She seems hungry for books and a little peace and quiet.'

Sister Harcourt looked at the address on the chart. It was the address of a flat in a high rise-block of apartments not far from the hospital, from whence a number of patients from problem families came cheerfully and with monotonous regularity to the hospital.

'They use Beatties as a kind of refuge and us as confessors,' said Sister Kaye Harcourt with a sigh. 'If we weren't here, they would need another prop to help them cope with life. I think we had Michelle's brother Damian in with impetigo when I was here two years ago.' She smiled. 'Damian conjures up a handsome embryo film star type, but Michelle's brother was a thin, undernourished little boy with a squint that was rectified when the impetigo was cleared up. Fancy names often compensate for the lack of other material goodies.'

A soft warmth began to fill Kaye's heart. Dear old Beattie's was the same, scooping up the sick and among them many underprivileged and inadequate families who turned to the sympathetic staff for comfort, advice or just a contact with the outside world. Memories of the old days flooded back as they walked from bed to bed in the main ward, looking down at sleeping children, peeping between shut cubicle curtains to see dressings and to smile at apprehensive new-comers who had never seen the inside of a hospital and found the strange smells and sounds confusing and vaguely frightening.

'Shall I let the T's and A's sit in the day room until the house surgeon comes to go over their chests before tomorrow's list, Sister? Two are a bit tearful as Mum had to go home to cope with the rest of the family. You'd think that twins would be company for each other but this pair seem to want to punch and pinch and show no signs of brotherly love!' Staff Nurse Benson laughed. 'They might be better watching telly for an hour.'

'They can stay there until supper or until the doctor comes. Who is on the firm now?'

'The house surgeon is a Nigerian doctor called Charumbera, and he's great with the tinies. He helps with the ENT list and should be here this evening. The house physician is Tony Smythe, God's gift to junior nurses.' Nurse Benson blushed. 'Sorry, Sister. Actually, he's good too. He leaves the firm in three months, time and likes working here so much that he's applied for a job at Great Ormond Street.'

'And the senior men or women?' Nurse Benson saw the new Sister tense her hand on the chart she held. 'Is Dr Hanley still here?'

'Yes. He's almost at retiring age but he works twice as hard as any doctor I know. He was the one who helped to start the research for Maple Syrup Syndrome, in conjuction with Great Ormond Street and other leading British hospitals. He has the usual large retinue of registrars following him everywhere, some from other hospitals looking in on his work and some from Beattie's and, just lately, because so much interest has been shown in the pituitary investigation, overseas students and consultants. It makes bed-making a bit fraught at times, Sister. They descend on the ward like locusts and leave it as if a tornado had hit it.'

'I do know,' said Sister Harcourt. 'I gave up being annoyed a long time ago.' She half smiled, as if her thoughts were slightly bitter. 'I gave up being up-tight about a lot of things,' she said softly. 'It's as well to get everything into perspective in a ward full of sick children. Just carry on as you have been doing for the next few days and I'll keep a low profile unless something happens that I can't ignore.'

'Thank you, Sister.' Nurse Benson looked relieved. 'They said that . . .' She patted the head of a huge teddy bear sitting at the end of a cot and bent down to tuck the blanket round the child lying there. 'This is little Min, who is recovering from an appendicectomy done two days ago. You're a very good girl, aren't you, dear?' The child smiled and sucked her thumb, gazing up at the new Sister with round eyes. 'This is Sister. She's come to look after us,' said Nurse Benson and walked to the next cot.

'They said what, Nurse Benson?' Sister Harcourt asked as they went back to the office. The nurse stared as if she couldn't make out what her superior meant. 'In the ward you were about to pass on a handed-down opinion of me. I doubt if there is anyone but Casualty Sister and Dr Hanley who remember that I was here.'

'It was nothing.' The girl was embarrassed. 'Dr Hanley was teasing me, and saying that you were very strict.'

'He's right.' Kaye's tone was crisp. 'I am realistic about tidiness, but when it comes to the work that matters, you will find that what he said is true.' She smiled, taking away the sharpness of her words. 'I shall have to re-establish my reputation.'

Nurse Benson went away to change the two

babies in the far cots and Sister Harcourt opened the shabby book that had once been a part of her work and routine. Dr Ben Hanley had two pages and another taped in as his space was used up. She read the early entries and his preferences for certain drugs and dressings for the children under his care—and later, the more scientific notes, with names of the medical scientists working with him, and the telephone numbers and addresses of their laboratories.

She turned the pages and stopped at one name, her heart betraying her with sensations that she thought were dead. Surely, after two years, she could read his name without this tightening of her facial muscles and a dull numb pain of bitter remembrance? Dr Orson Latimer. The name danced before her and seemed to dominate the page. It was over, quite over, and she had her life to live, back in the hospital that she loved and yet had once sworn that she would never enter again. Orson, with his thick, corn-gold hair and the unusual combination of dark eyelashes; Orson, with bright blue eyes that could bewitch and condemn.

Where was he now? She slammed the book shut and sent motes of dust through the ray of sunshine gilding her desk. What did it matter where Orson Latimer had gone after he left Beattie's? He had gone back home to America and by now must be well and truly married, or at least living with someone on a permanent basis. Kaye looked out of the window. It was just the shock of the familiar room and the unchanged atmosphere of the ward. Everything changes, they say, she thought, and yet nothing had changed. They say . . . There it was again. I wonder what it was they said? she thought, believing nothing of her staff nurse's explanation. Who was there at Beattie's who recalled the events that led to the heartbroken staff nurse leaving to go North to strangers and a midwifery course?

The morning routine went smoothly as this was not an operation day, and by the time she went down to lunch, Sister Kaye Harcourt was once more glad to be back and beginning to know her small patients. She paused by the door of the old refectory, now streamlined into a cafeteria, and looked up, wondering how many even knew that the old beams were from the original priory hall used by nuns many years before it became a hospital with a reputation that grew and made the Princess Beatrice famous the world over.

Kaye collected soup and ham salad and looked round for a vacant table. She stopped, the stirrings of her earlier unease threatening again. Oh, no, it wasn't possible!

'Hello, Harcourt. I heard you were coming back.' The hard blue eyes searched her face for some hint of reaction.

'Hello, March. I thought you were in India.'

'I did go.' Brenda March moved her cloak from the chair opposite her own, and there was no alternative for Sister Harcourt, other than cutting the woman completely, but to sit down. She bent to sip her soup and hoped that she seemed hungry and preoccupied with the food.

'You went to Edinburgh.' It wasn't a question but the beginning of a list of everything that Sister March recalled about her. She was Sister March

now, not the senior staff nurse in Male Orthopaedics. With what relish she must have told the
story of the pale little nurse leaving because she had
fallen in love with the American who came and
dallied a little, loved a lot and left many torn
emotions and badly cracked hearts among the
nurses in training. It had caused quite a flutter at
the time, but was soon forgotten by everyone—
except the woman with the computer-like brain and
no heart. Kaye Harcourt glanced at Brenda March
as she went to fetch her pudding, and wondered if
the cool blonde was as indifferent to men as she
made out.

At the time, Nurse March had been indignant
about men in general and Orson Latimer in particular. She had no time for love—or sex, which she
insisted was the only thing that men wanted. And
yet she had managed to be there when Orson
quarrelled with Kaye and rumour had it that
Brenda had offered him the comfort that Kaye
refused him. It was ridiculous. She had made it
clear that Orson was a loose-living, selfish animal,
taking what he wanted even if he destroyed it in the
process. But things could change a lot in two years.

Kaye Harcourt watched her come back to her
seat. What had been so good between the golden
boy and the dark quiet nurse had soured and ended
in bitter acrimony, but only after Brenda March
had appeared on the scene with her snide remarks
and sniggering innuendoes. There had been
nothing definite, but when she left a room, March
left behind an atmosphere of tension and growing
distrust, causing friction and the airing of words
that were best unspoken.

What had Brenda hinted, way back in those distant times that were only two years away? First, she had let it out, quite by accident, that Kaye Harcourt was secretly engaged to be married to an old school friend and spent weekends with him in a cosy cottage in Surrey. It had enough truth to make explanations difficult. Vincent Burgess had known Kaye at school and was fond of her in a brotherly way—and glad to make use of her when he entertained business colleagues and needed a hostess. But he had a resident housekeeper and there was no hint of anything more than warm affection between himself and Kaye.

Kaye stared at Brenda's glossy head under the crisp, frilled cap of a Sister at Beattie's and wondered if she recalled her own sly manoeuvres. She had built up Orson as a lecher who went with anyone he could if Kaye wasn't available, and then the inevitable explosion came, with Kaye going to Edinburgh and Orson back to the States.

Kaye Harcourt smiled. That must have been a shock. Surely Brenda March could have arranged it better? Or had Orson seen through the blonde nurse's scheming too late to make amends with Kaye? She collected a strawberry mousse and went back to the table.

'So here we are, back again as if we had never been away,' she said lightly.

Sister March darted a look of dislike which she tried to hide in a sigh.

'Where did you go after I left?' said Kaye. 'Or have you been keeping an eye on Beattie's ever since?'

The old rancour gave way to curiosity and she

was glad to find that she could face this woman with a half-smile, as if nothing in the past mattered. Brenda had done her worst, and nothing that she could dream up would make any impression now that a hard shell of self-protection lay round Kaye's heart.

'I went on holiday for a month and then worked in India: Wales, too, for a time, doing agency work.' Sister March twisted the bow under her chin as if it irritated her. 'Then I saw the orthopaedic job vacant and came back.' She spoke rapidly, as if she wanted to keep her own affairs private.

'A month away on holiday? How self-indulgent. Where did you go?' Kaye Harcourt didn't have any interest in the answer until she saw the dull colour rising in the woman's cheeks. 'Somewhere good? The continent? Spain?'

'No, actually I had friends I wanted to visit. They asked me to go and I've refused many times.' She toyed with her coffee-cup, turning it round in the saucer as if looking for a label. A suspicion dawned and Kaye continued to look as if she expected more details. 'I have friends in Boston and Maine,' said Brenda March, almost defiantly.

'I see.' There was a fraught moment of silence. 'I've never been across the Atlantic. Did you fly? It must be fun to go on the QE II, but not alone.' It was almost a question, but one she didn't want to ask.

'I went alone and met my friends there.' Brenda pushed the cup and saucer away quickly and rose to her feet, smoothing down the well-cut uniform dress in the dark green fabric that was still a jealously guarded right of the senior staff of the

Princess Beatrice, even though mutterings from the Ministry urged conformity with other less well-known hospitals. The juniors wore the new regulation clothes but longed for the privilege of wearing the dignified and graceful dresses and caps supplied when they reached the dizzy heights of Staff Nurse and beyond.

Sister Harcourt glanced at the tiny Victorian watch pinned to her breast pocket and decided that she must go back to the ward. She was surprised to find Sister March lingering in the corridor and then walking with her as far as the main staircase. 'Are you busy?' said Kaye, finding the silence oppressive.

'Busy enough to be interesting. Why did you come back to Children's? I should have thought you had enough of that ward when you were here last.'

'I missed them,' said Sister Harcourt simply. 'I like the work and love the children and there was nothing to prevent me coming back.'

'Nothing?'

'I can think of no reason for me to work some-where away from London, where most of my friends are, and to work in any other hospital but this one. Two years and a hectic midwifery course were enough to show me what I wanted to do with my life.' Kaye walked briskly to the lift. 'I am going straight back to the second floor. Coming?'

'No. I have someone to see.' Sister March stepped back as if she had only then changed her mind. Their two wards were on the same long corridor, one at each end, with Men's Medical in between and a central station for a medical secretary, with facilities for doctors to study and write notes in a deep alcove once used as a store. The lift sighed and halted and Sister Harcourt opened the door.

What had March wanted to say? She must be curious to know if I have ever been in touch with Orson, Kaye thought, and somewhere in that sleek blonde head was a question or even a piece of news that she found it difficult to keep to herself. Kaye Harcourt shrugged, as if to throw off the clinging veil of hostility that the blonde woman draped over her. It was all in the past and nothing that Brenda March could say or do would have any effect on her.

The muted sound of children talking and laughing came from the day room and Kaye smiled. The first impact of the ward was over, and so was the fact that she had handled the book in which the familiar name was written, together with the serious account of his likes and dislikes and the addition of semi-facetious remarks that accompanied most names, written in different inks and in many handwritings. She knew that she had added some herself. Orson was a Taurean, and she had drawn a skittish calf knocking over a pile of dishes. But calves grew up into stubborn bulls who charge towards anything they want or hate. He had been stubborn, but fair. His stubborn streak had given him the tenacity to fight all night for the life of a child that most would have given up as hopeless. Kaye's eyes filled with tears. No, she must forget that even broad-shouldered American rugger players with proud, arrogant heads could be gentle, with the touching gentleness of the really strong.

Nurse Benson was waiting to go to lunch. 'Dr Hanley was on the phone, Sister. He is coming in later with some visiting doctors to take notes about the PHS children. He is building up yet another team, this time for that one syndrome, and some of his new people will be sleeping in the new place up the road.' She smiled. 'He's a pet. He asked me if I was available tonight to give them coffee and to make them feel at home, and to ask some other staff nurses to help me. He says that his wife will be in later with a tray of snacks and if you are free, she wants to see you.'

'Jill Hanley? That will be nice. I promised myself I'd ring her as soon as I got settled in. She's the same as ever?'

'Still plump and smiling and grumbling at Dr Hanley about working too hard. He says he might retire in a couple of years, but I can't believe it and neither can she.'

'Go to lunch, Nurse, and you can check with whoever is off this evening and likely to help you. From the notes and my morning round, I can't see that you need hurry back. I shall stay until you return. I'll work in the office getting to know more details about the patients.'

'Thank you, Sister. I was talking to Dr Charumbera and he says that he knows two of the men coming here, so he will be there this evening. He lives in the new block and is very helpful.'

'I see I have a lot of new faces to meet. In the dining-room I saw some that must be new to Beatties. I also saw Sister March, who was here as a staff nurse in my time.'

Kaye looked at the pleasant, open face of Nurse

Benson, who made a rather obvious grimace at the sound of the name. 'Have you worked with bones?'

'Not yet, and I don't think I want to.' Nurse Benson picked up her bag. 'Can I go now, Sister?'

'Yes, of course.' Kaye watched her go and wondered if March had a reputation from the old days or had come back as hard and unrelenting with her staff as she had been as a staff nurse. Time and experience should mellow her and show that discipline can be kept and good service expected from nurses without having to bully them into a mass of accident-prone jelly.

Kaye went into the office and looked at the drug list. Most of the usual ones were there, but some new proprietary ones had been added and she noted them in the tiny book in which she kept anything that she might forget or need for reference. She straightened the papers on the desk and went into the side ward. The little girl there was concentrating on a simple jigsaw puzzle.

'Hello, Michelle. May I come in?' The child looked up and seemed to wake up to her surroundings. 'Is that a very difficult puzzle?' Michelle nodded, but put an arm round the board as if to stop anyone from seeing it. 'And you want to do it all alone? With no help so that you can know it is yours?' said Sister gently.

Michelle nodded and relaxed. 'It's mine,' she said.

'And you like it in here alone?'

'They can't take it away from me. They can't break it and throw it away.'

'You think they might? Do your brothers and sisters do that?' The child nodded and her face seemed to grow smaller.

'My brother does.'

'I expect your mum and dad stop him.' Michelle shook her head. The bruises on her cheek and the abrasions on her hands were almost gone and from the chart she was even putting on weight in the short time she had been in the ward.

'I don't have a sister. They took her away.'

'Why was that?' There was nothing in the notes to hint at a child dying in the family. Michelle bent her head and put a piece of the puzzle in place, and Sister Harcourt knew that she had shut her mind to more questions.

'When you have finished that, we'll put it carefully on the shelf where no one can touch and you can come and watch television with the others.' Michelle glanced at the shelf, assessing its safety. 'I promise it will be all right. You can finish it tomorrow if you like.' Michelle smiled with sudden sweetness. 'You can watch all the programmes for children and when your mum comes to see you, you can tell her what you have seen.'

'No,' said Michelle. 'I don't want her to know.' She turned back to the puzzle and ignored Sister Harcourt. Something was wrong. Most children looked forward to daily visits. Kaye called a junior nurse and asked if Michelle had many visitors.

'No, Sister. Nurse Benson was saying at report last night that she must make sure she doesn't feel left out. Her mother has three boys to look after and she says she can't get here very often.'

'Three boys but no other girl?' Sister frowned. 'There is another sister, who "went away" according to Michelle. Did she die or was she fostered?'

'Nurse Benson said that one child was in Care, and the social worker is coming to see you today, Sister.'

'I see.' Kaye thought of the thin child in the lonely side room who preferred to be there rather than in the more human atmosphere of the ward, and hoped that the social worker could provide some reason for Michelle's withdrawal apart from the fact that she might be self-conscious about her fast-fading scars.

The new admissions were brightening and laughing at a cartoon programme in the day room. Nothing inhibited about them, thought Kaye Harcourt. Another day and they would become difficult to keep quiet. There were a few empty beds and one empty side ward, and she decided to keep Michelle in the other side ward for a day or so unless the room was badly needed. She so obviously enjoyed the solitude after a crowded and noisy existence at home. Kaye made a mental note to put a card on the other room door to tell the medical team that their patients were in there now.

A curtained cot stood at the end of the ward near the office and the intravenous drip was slowly releasing its life-giving fluid into the badly dehydrated baby who had been rushed in the day before, having been abandoned in the holiday camp a few miles away on the river. Only the sharp ears of a cleaner had heard the sound of the child whimpering and even now there was a risk that he was too ill to recover.

Gently, Kaye Harcourt moistened the dry lips with saline and glucose solution and pulled back the bedclothes to make sure that the tiny arms and legs were not developing sores from pressure. She noted with satisfaction that the baby was being nursed on a natural sheepskin and wondered where the Australian doctor who introduced the idea to the ward had gone. At such times it was impossible to be completely objective and she longed to take the baby into her arms and to love him.

His chart was settling well and his respirations were back to normal. He stirred and grunted and when Kaye felt for the soft spot on his head that is depressed when a baby lacks fluid, she knew that he was recovering.

As she walked the ward, she made notes and listed names so that at report she would know every detail about her charges. It was a part of her early training that now made her work easier as she could take in such details and remember them perfectly.

The twins, who had by now talked to the last batch of children who had already been relieved of their tonsils and adenoids and would go home in the morning, were demanding their tonsils to take home with them, but she would make no promises. If, when they were removed, they were found to be very infected, then little fingers might break the bottle containing the gory souvenirs and spread streptococcal infection. But if they were merely enlarged and no longer infected, then perhaps an unbreakable plastic container might be found for them, so that the twins could boast about their time in hospital to their envious friends.

Visitors came and went through the afternoon and Sister Harcourt went off duty for a while, more confident now that she knew the ward and looking forward to returning in time to let Nurse Benson off for the evening. If it could be like this, the future would be pleasant, even happy.

She made tea in the freshly-painted kitchen of the new block and admired the pretty covers in the large sitting-room where the nurses would entertain the visiting team this evening. She smiled. When she began her training at Beattie's there were sisters who still clung to the idea that it was immoral for nurses to have men in the nurses' home. And now, doctors and male nurses and visiting surgeons slept in the same house, in rooms adjoining the ones in which nurses lived, and there was no restriction on the time of nurses reporting back from off duty.

'Harcourt!' Kaye turned to face the beaming West Indian girl who dropped her two suitcases on the floor and rushed to hug her. 'I heard you were coming back, girl, and I wasn't here to greet you.'

'I thought you went home!'

'So I did, but I couldn't keep away.' She gave a deep throaty laugh that seemed to warm the room. 'I went home to my family and met a guy from St Phillip's in Middlesex. I go all the way across the ocean only to come back to be near him, and now I'm down the road from you in Men's Medical! It's a crazy world. We're going to be married in three or four months as soon as he knows his fellowship results.'

'It's wonderful to see you, Ercil. Don't tell me they made you a Sister too? They must be hard up to upgrade the two of us.'

'Sure they did. I am now Sister Ercil Kingston and loving every minute. What about you? How is your love life?'

'Completely negative,' said Kaye, laughing. It was funny but Ercil could ask the most impertinent questions and never gave offence.

'C'mon now. With your lovely face and figure, you can't tell me that somewhere there isn't a man mad about you?'

'I can and do. I went off men a long time ago.'

'You mean since Orson?' The girl stared. 'That's bad. What about the other nice guy that March smeared with her own nasty brand of lies? Vincent, wasn't it?'

'He's just the same, bless him. We meet and enjoy dinner together, or I go there when he has friends to a meal, but never in a million years could we get married.' Kaye sighed. 'I wonder if I did the right thing coming back here? I saw March in the dining-room and she might be a thorn in the flesh.'

'If it's all over, what does she matter? She can't hurt you now you know her for what she is. It *is* all over?' The concerned brown eyes were thoughtful.

'Of course. It was all over before I left Beattie's. I shall never see him again and he must have forgotten me by now.'

'I sure hope you're right, honey.' Ercil picked up her bags. 'See you later. I have a date with my man. He met me at the airport after my visit home but had to go back for a ward round. I just have time to change and take a taxi to meet him for dinner.' Ercil rushed away, leaving Kaye with the afterglow of her good humour and friendliness. I have one friend here, she thought, and went back to the ward smiling happily.

'Sister?'

'Are you ready to go off duty?' Sister Harcourt

smiled at her staff nurse. 'Have a good evening—
and I might look in at the party when I come off
duty.'

'Sister, the team is here with Dr Hanley. They
are in the side ward talking to the two children for
PHS tests and the parents are there too. I asked
Nurse to make coffee. Is that all right?'

'Fine. I'll go in at once unless you have anything
urgent to report.'

'It's all in the book, Sister. No change.' Nurse
Benson hurried away with the impetus of one who
has been called back too many times to assume that
today she would get off quickly, and Sister
Harcourt went quietly into the big side ward which
seemed crowded with people.

Dr Hanley was talking to a woman with tired
eyes and anxious lines on a face that should have
looked younger. Other men in white coats stood
talking in low voices, but mostly listening to one
man who dominated the room.

He paused in mid-sentence, as if sensing another
presence in the room, and as Kaye Harcourt leaned
against the hard rim of a bed-table for support, with
her hand to her throat and her eyes dark and full of
tragic awareness, he saw her and forgot what he
was saying.

It could have been no more than a moment that
cut time into sharply defined past and present, but
it seemed as if two years had evaporated from the
record books and been removed from memory.

'Ah, Sister Harcourt. How good to think that
you will be looking after our children again.'

Dr Hanley beamed and held out his hand. She
put her own into it and he wondered at the lifeless

coldness of the smooth skin, so unlike the vibrant girl he had known when she was working with him two years earlier. He saw that the man with deep golden hair was staring at her.

'I was forgetting. You know each other. I was going to introduce you to the leader of my team, Dr Orson Latimer, but I expect you knew that he was coming back for a while?'

'No, I didn't know. Hello, Dr Latimer,' said the new sister. The words came from her lips with ease and her normally pale cheeks held an under-glow that lit her face. The green uniform seemed to enhance the dark fire in her eyes and the fine, delicate whiteness of her cap and bow gave an almost nun-like fragility and dignity that Orson Latimer had never seen in the woman he had once loved.

He took a step towards her but the room was full and she seemed to recede as if rejecting any physical contact, so their hands didn't touch. They came no closer than half a room away and perhaps no other person knew that the air was torn and that the pain of lost moments, forgotten vows and the cries of dying love were there between them, demanding recognition.

'Hello, Sister. You look well in green,' he said formally. 'It must be over a year,' he went on, and she knew that he remembered as well as she did that it was longer than that.

'Probably,' she said. 'I've been away doing other things and time flashes by when one is happy.'

'You enjoyed midwifery?' Dr Hanley asked. 'All good experience, but you're needed here, eh, Latimer? Nice that you know each other's work as you'll be seeing the team a lot during the next week or so, Sister.'

'It sounds an interesting project,' said Kaye and picked up her clipboard with the notes for the tests. 'Perhaps you would like to confer in my office while the parents stay with the children and put them to bed?' She smiled. 'Stay until they settle and Nurse will bring you some coffee.'

One or two of the team introduced themselves and she had already met the house surgeon and house physician, and when they got to her office Orson Latimer stood on the other side of the room, hemmed in by his colleagues while she handed out coffee and Dr Hanley explained what would happen in the tests.

'I've contacted the medical scientists who will take the blood and urine tests and keep graphs after the meat extract is given. Both children have been measured today, I believe, and will come to Outpatients after they leave for regular height measurements. We shall gather a lot of data with the steady flow of children coming in for tests, and then we can follow-up their hormone replacement if we find they are suitable for treatment.'

He looks the same except for his eyes. And were those lines there round his mouth when he is not smiling? Were they engraved by worry, too much work or just self-indulgence? Kaye wondered, seeing Orson's firm shoulders and slim waist; she found it difficult to believe that he had been guilty of physical neglect. He must have a wife or a lover. She swallowed hard. She could never ask anyone. What if he had brought someone with him from the States, a rippling blonde who would enchant all the

other men and make them envious? Would she
meet this other woman?

Kaye Harcourt tried to free her mind. She was
jumping to too many conclusions. What did it
matter if he was here? They had worked together in
complete harmony in the past and now she was no
longer in love with him and he would have every
nubile girl in the place running after him in ten
minutes flat, so she need never see him off duty.

'I'm sorry, Dr Hanley, I wasn't thinking.'

'I only wanted to know if you had seen my wife
yet. She is coming to pick me up and leave some
things for this evening.'

'If you don't need me here, I'll ring down to the
main hall. She might even be in the duty room
here.'

Kaye left the office thankfully. It was only when
she found herself alone in the corridor that she
began to tremble. Pull yourself together, she told
herself angrily. He is nothing to you and you are
nothing to him. She heard a child crying and
listened. It was a cry of utter desolation and
came from the second side ward. Slipping softly
into the room, she saw Michelle lying huddled at
the foot of the bed, the bedclothes all on the floor.
The soft light from the night lamp showed the
tears on her face and the small body shaking with
sobs.

Sister Harcourt picked her up and caught a
blanket to put round her as Michelle clung to the
soft shoulder of the woman who thought she had no
feelings left. The sobs subsided and the little girl
nuzzled against the soft breast, finding security and
peace. Kaye looked up and saw a man standing in

the doorway watching her. The soft light lit a glow in her eyes and the child was now still.

'Jill Hanley is in your office, Sister.' His voice was harsh and his anger bubbled like some sleeping geyser, sensed but not seen on the surface. 'When you're ready; I'll tell her you got held up.' He stared at the woman within her own wall of peace. 'Hell, Kaye, you always did look like a damned madonna,' he said—and was gone.

CHAPTER TWO

THE SOUNDS from the sitting-room faded as Sister Kaye Harcourt slowly went up the stairs to her room in the new block of apartments for staff, just up the road from the hospital. It was only eleven o'clock but she felt as if she had been up for days. She tried to believe her weariness was because the first day in any job was rather trying, even when everything went right and her staff were helpful, but she knew that the tension she felt was because the past had erupted and shocked her into knowing that she still had some feeling left for Dr Orson Latimer.

Only the fact that she was surrounded by the doctors in Dr Ben Hanley's new team had made it possible to remain calm and to manage to avoid all contact with the handsome American. Ben Hanley was flattering in his delight at having her back at Beattie's and several of the new men had eyed her with definite approval. And when Jill Hanley arrived and cornered Kaye to talk about old times, when she had been a sister in the gynae ward and the new nurse first arrived from preliminary training school shaking with fright and yet showing early promise, she had almost forgotten that Orson Latimer was in the same room.

'Do you remember?' said Jill, laughing. 'I had to winkle you out of the sluice room and convince you that every patient you touched wouldn't die!'

31

'You were wonderful. I think that if I had begun my training on any other ward, I'd have turned and run away during the first week.' Kaye smiled warmly, gradually relaxing as she had done at other times when under tension and the plump and pretty older woman had known instinctively that something was wrong. 'I think I model myself on you when I have new nurses on the ward.'

'Never! You have your own brand of sympathetic firmness. Ben notices these things, even if he is a bit vague about notes and X-rays at times.' Jill looked serious and glanced across the room where Orson Latimer was deep in conversation with her husband. 'Did you know he was here in England again?'

Kaye shook her head.

'You should have been warned.' Jill looked annoyed. 'Surely someone must have known, apart from Ben and me?' She frowned. 'In fact, he came home and said that one of the staff who knew you had offered to meet you before you came on duty and would put you in the picture. Otherwise *I'd* have given you a ring.'

'It's all right. It really is all right,' Kaye stressed. 'Two years is a long time and it's over for both of us. It might even be interesting to work together again. After the first meeting, which I admit was a bit of a shaker, I can look across at him and wonder what it was that we ever had all that time ago.' She could glimpse the bright head and the firm set of his shoulders and knew that as he became engrossed in what he was saying, his right forefinger would jab the air to accent a point he wanted to make.

'That's a relief. You have to see him on the ward

and Ben was hoping that you would come to one of our parties next week. Orson might well be there.' Jill searched Kaye's face for the truth. 'Can you do that?' Her face cleared. 'The obvious solution is for you to bring a friend. Wasn't there an old faithful lurking in the background when you were here at Beattie's the last time?'

'You mean Vincent? He's not an old faithful, unless you mean a very good friend. There was nothing between us in the old days and there is nothing now. We meet and have a very pleasant time together, but that's all. He has been in love twice and each time it broke up—I have helped him when he had to entertain his business associates but there has never been the "tea and sympathy" thing.' She looked pensive. 'I'll think about it, Jill, but it might not be a good idea. Vincent was a bit up-tight about Orson. It was like having a brother ready to bloody the nose of the man who upset his sister!'

'You *must* come. One of the others in the team would be delighted to bring you, judging by the looks you are getting,' Jill insisted.

'I could even come alone. I'm a big girl now, Jill.' Kaye saw that Ben Hanley was looking at her. 'Nice to see you again. Jot your telephone number and address on the pad there and I'll be in touch. I think that your husband wants some attention, so I'd better look efficient.'

She walked towards the consultant and gave him the clipboard. 'Are those the acceptable deviation curves?' he said.

'Yes. It certainly saved time to have the parents here when the children were admitted. The chil-

dren settled quickly and the team could ask questions and take the height and weight of the parents
for reference. Dr Smythe said that the first parts of
the curve are ready with the history of growth so
far.' To her relief, Dr Hanley was alone apart from
the smiling Nigerian doctor who was so interested
in the study of endocrine deficiency in children.

'It makes everything much clearer, sir,' said Dr
Charumbera. 'The father of Bobbie was small until
he was twelve and then grew rapidly to five feet
seven—not tall, but certainly not too short to be a
problem. His father before him was short and the
mother isn't very big.'

'How old is Bobbie?' Ben Hanley looked at the
chart. 'You think they are over-reacting because he
has been outgrown by his contemporaries at
school? I see that he is eight now. We'll give him the
Bovril test and if it is even slightly on the positive
side, I suggest we keep him under observation but
do nothing for a while.' They walked slowly along
to the side ward where the two children sat playing
with Lego bricks at the table. The parents had
gone. 'What about the others?'

Dr Charumbera consulted the notes. 'Father
almost six feet and mother five-seven, and Michael
is ten. He looks kinda small, I think.'

'He does show all the signs,' said Dr Hanley.
'We'll do the tests and they can go into the general
ward when the next batch come in. If we keep a
steady stream of likely candidates it will help with
the comparisons and they won't feel odd when they
know that several other children are in for the same
thing. Some of the mothers get a bit worried if they
think their infant is the only one with something as

obscure as this condition.'

He gave the clipboard back to Sister Harcourt. 'I'd like to do a round now, if I may. I haven't seen all my patients today and we can't neglect the rest of the ward just because we have such fascinating projects under way.'

They went into the ward and Kaye Harcourt told him about Michelle. As soon as she had fallen asleep, after Orson Latimer appeared in the doorway, the new Sister had closed the door gently and told the nurse on duty to peep in every half an hour in case she had another bad dream.

'Shall we leave Michelle until last? She seemed upset after a nightmare, but she is sleeping peacefully now.'

Kaye Harcourt could almost hear Orson Latimer's tense voice again, hard with sharp dislike and irritation that he had to speak to her again on any subject at all, and was reminded that he thought her false beneath the facade of cool dark calm. He still hates me, she thought. 'It was good to meet Jill again,' she said, pushing away old sorrows and determined to forget.

'She was thrilled to think you would be here.' Ben Hanley stopped by a bed where a child lay, flung out on the cover, sound asleep and rosy-cheeked. 'Nice that you still have a few friends here, Sister. When I asked Sister March to tell you that Orson was back, she was delighted. I had forgotten that you and she were old chums until she reminded me and offered to welcome you.'

'It was good of you to think of it,' said Kaye. The least said about March, the better for all concerned. She was just the same devious bitch who had caused the trouble between Orson and Kaye all that time ago and there was no point in bringing that misery back to the surface again. But it was a warning to keep away from the cool blonde woman and to let her know nothing of her private affairs. How March must have relished the thought of Kaye Harcourt meeting Orson Latimer unexpectedly in a public situation.

'This child is going home tomorrow, I think. She was in the day room most of the time I was on duty so I know very little about her,' Kaye explained.

'Ah, yes. This is Helen. She fell down in the school playground and we had to take out half the gravel from the driveway that was embedded in her shins. She had anti-tetanus and a bad reaction to it as her mother failed to tell the casualty officer that she had had the injections only a month earlier after a wood splinter in her arm turned septic and had to be removed. That was in another hospital and we had no way of knowing that she had no need for further anti-tetanus. I think we shall see her again. Some children can't keep out of trouble, can they? She looks the picture of health but decidedly accident-prone. I wish they all had such lovely colour.'

He gazed down at the sleeping child and his voice was affectionate. Kaye was reminded that he and Jill had no family and knew that it was a sadness that even his work with children could never quite erase.

They went from bed to bed and finally arrived at the side ward in time to see the nurse peeping in to check. 'Asleep?' said Dr Hanley. The nurse nodded and smiled.

'Did she have a visitor this evening, Nurse?' Kaye asked.

'No, Sister. Dr Charumbera, Nurse Benson asked me to tell you that we couldn't get in touch with the parents—and she is due to be discharged in a day or so, isn't she?'

'She should go home, but I wanted you to see her first, sir,' said the house surgeon. 'She is very nervous of men.' He laughed. 'Except me. Being black, she doesn't see me as the same as the men in her life, so she feels safe.'

'Have you learned anything new?' Dr Hanley enquired.

'No, she refuses to talk about her father and mother. The social worker came in when you were off duty, Sister, but I saw her. There is another girl in Care and the father likes only boys. Shall I send her out and risk another assault or shall we keep her in for a while until we can talk to the parents, sir?' The young doctor waited for advice.

'If we have a bed, keep her in—but she should mix with the other children and gain confidence.' Dr Hanley walked back to the office and found it empty. 'Did Latimer go?'

'The big American?' The nurse's eyes sparkled. 'He went with the others over to the new block with the food that Mrs Hanley brought.' Kaye smiled. It still took Orson Latimer just five minutes to make his mark on the females of any place he entered, and two years had done nothing to blur his impact. 'Are you going over to the party, Sister?'

It was after the time when the new Sister should have been off duty and the night nurses had already finished their first round. 'I might look in,' Kaye said, unwilling to seem either anxious to go to meet the new team again, or indifferent, as she sensed the envy in the girl's manner. What it was to be starry-eyed about a few new faces—or about one in particular! I feel a hundred and twenty and sexless with it, thought Kaye.

She gathered her folder and cloak and made her way down to the main entrance. The drive was freshly surfaced and the antiseptic smell of new tar made her sniff with appreciation. Was a royal visit on the programme in the coming weeks? Fresh drives and new paint usually meant that they were out to impress some VIP.

The tail lights of a line of cars moved slowly up the hill away from the hospital and Kaye thought that it was busier than it had been two years ago. Would everything here be compared with those former days? Was there no way that she could ever be free of the past? It had seemed dead, but was it now stirring like some great sleeping monster, to unsettle her heart and perhaps even to destroy it?

In the hall she met Tony Smythe, who was on his way to the smart new kitchen to put coffee to filter. 'I have to keep sober as I'm on call, Sister. Come and have some coffee. You don't want to get mixed up with that crowd in there.'

He grinned cheerfully and Kaye followed him into the bright room, glad to have an excuse to miss the party and Orson Latimer. Tony produced a packet of chocolate mints filched from the party. 'You now know one of my many weaknesses,' he said. The water was boiling and he poured it over the ground coffee. 'Another of my weaknesses is lovely women with smooth dark hair,' he said.

'I bet you tell that to all the blondes,' she said, laughing.

'There are too many blondes about,' he said. 'I can think of a few here who send shudders up and down my spine—and not because I'm thrilled.'

'Don't tell me. You think I remind you of your mother!'

He looked hurt. 'I just look too young,' he said. 'Just because you have a dignified uniform, it doesn't mean you are older than me. In any case, I prefer older women.'

If only you knew how young you look, trying to chat me up with all the lack of expertise that girls never notice when they are seventeen, twenty, or whenever they fall in love for the first time, Kaye thought. 'Is that coffee ready, or shall I go into the party?' she said.

'Don't go in there. The new bloke is holding court with every female drooling over him. Stay and tell me the story of your life. And first of all, what is your name?'

'I'm Kaye off duty, but never on the ward. This is very good coffee, Tony.' She perched on a bar stool by the breakfast extension and he sat on the other side, gazing at her. 'I'll have some of those very up-market chocolates too, if I can't go and join the harem.'

'You know him, don't you?' Tony put down his cup. 'Sister March said something but I was in a hurry and didn't have time to get the whole picture.'

'He was here two years ago when I was in the ward as a senior staff nurse. I went to do midder and he left for the States and this is the first time we've met since then.'

Kaye heard her own voice, flat and uninterested, and knew that this conversation might have to be repeated often before the half-remembered rumours had a decent burial. 'Orson Latimer was always very attractive to women and I see that he hasn't lost his touch.' She laughed and was amazed how easy it was to sound amused. 'Everyone had a mild crush on him in those days, even me.'

'And you aren't rushing in to renew old times?'

'Hardly. Two years is much too long to have the same likes and dislikes. I hope I've progressed since then. He's a very good doctor,' she conceded.

'He's been studying paediatrics in the States, I believe.' Tony grinned. 'Nice to know that we have some things in the UK that the Yanks haven't done. They talk about all the wonders of American surgery, but quietly they are doing marvellous things at Great Ormond Street and at Beattie's that haven't seen the light of day over there.'

'Do I sense a trace of prejudice? My aunt used to be very anti-American after being jilted by a soldier in the war. What did they say?'

'Over-paid, over-sexed and over here?' said Tony with relish.

'Trust you to know that one! Well, I have to go now. I think I've just about enough energy to have a bath and to look out a fresh uniform for tomorrow and then I shall sleep like the dead.' She smiled. 'Nice to meet you, Tony. The new projects sound good.' She gathered her things together and made for the door, silently blessing the fresh-faced houseman for giving her the excuse to miss the party.

'I doubt if anyone will have missed me, but if they do, tell them that I was late off duty, had coffee with you and was too late and tired to join them.' Kaye walked up to her room and closed the door after her, taking her cap from its strings and carefully putting her dress on a hanger before running her bath. It was like living in a sleek hotel room with her own bathroom, and was a far cry from the shabby old rooms in the Victorian houses made over to the staff after the hostel and early training school burned down several years earlier.

She brushed out the long sleek dark hair and thrust it under a shower cap, and after her shower let it fall in a soft swathe on her shoulders. She wished that she had brought some of the coffee to her room, as now she was not so tired and the thought of reading in bed with another hot drink beside her was increasingly attractive. As if to encourage her in this, someone tapped on the door and called her name.

'Telephone!' they said, and ran back to the stairs without saying who was calling. Kaye looked at her watch. Who would ring at nearly midnight? She grabbed her dressing-gown and slippers and went to the telephone, her hair floating back on the pale blue gown and her feet thrust into the velvet mules with feathery pom-poms of silk that matched the gown.

'Sister Kaye Harcourt,' she said, slightly out of breath. 'Vincent! How nice to hear from you.'

'I tried earlier,' said the pleasant masculine voice, 'but you were still on duty. I listened to some music and thought you might be awake. How did it go?'

'Fine,' she said convincingly. It was essential to make Vincent think that going back to Beattie's was a success in every way. He had advised her to go anywhere but Beattie's if she came back to London and had grave doubts about her settling down happily in a hospital where she had been so unhappy and heart-broken.

The children are great and Ben Hanley is the same as ever. We have some very interesting projects under way and I think we shall get along fine.' She paused, wondering if she sounded over-enthusiastic. 'I'm tired now, but the first few days are like that when there are so many new faces to recall and all the various treatments and drugs to pin-point.'

Vincent sounded more cheerful and rambled on about the concert he had attended and the one to which he wanted her to go with him when she had time off next week. 'It's just the music you like, Kaye, and you know that good music relaxes you.'

'I'll try to make it, but as yet I haven't worked out my off-duty rota. It isn't fair to upset the schedule if my staff nurse has made arrangements for an existing one. You have this number and the hospital one if you need to leave a message. Have I got your latest office number? Wait a minute while I get a pen.'

She turned away from the phone to see if there was a ball-point pen in the lodge. It was hopeless putting a notepad and pencil by the phone as it disappeared each time and there was no way of making a note.

'Oh!' As she stepped back quickly, her foot caught on the instep of a man waiting behind her

and she stumbled. 'It's all right,' she said coolly as
Orson Latimer held her arm firmly to stop her
falling. 'Have you a pen?' she asked, hoping that he
would think her quickened breath was due to her
near accident. He handed her a gold-plated pen
and a small notepad, saying nothing and stepping
back as if the contact scalded him.

'I have a pen,' she said to Vincent and hardly
recognised her own handwriting as she put down
the address and telephone number of his new office
in the West End of London. 'Sounds very impressive,' she said, and hoped that Orson Latimer would
have gone before she finished talking. She glanced
back and he was looking at his wrist-watch in a very
definite way. Let him wait, she thought. Is he afraid
that she will be in bed and won't answer his call? He
sighed and it was impossible to concentrate any
longer.

'I have to go now. Someone is waiting to use the
phone. Good night, dear. See you very soon and I'll
ring about the concert.'

She turned and Orson stepped smartly to take
her place by the telephone. As she put the receiver
down it rang immediately, and she saw his face
soften and the mouth that once she had thought
held all the pleasures of paradise smile with gentle
love.

'Hello, honey. Thought I'd missed you. Someone hogged the phone for ages and I thought you
might give up.' His glance was hard and bright as if
he resented what he saw as Kaye walked slowly
away. He had not spoken to her at all, even when
he handed her the pen. She pushed the torn piece of
paper from the notepad into her pocket and froze.

She had taken his gold pen and put it in her pocket before tearing off her note and handing the pad back to him.

She paused by the stairs. He was still bent over the phone, his shoulders hunched as if to shut out everything but the sound and the vibes coming to him from . . . a woman, certainly, and a woman from outside the hospital. It was as Kaye had imagined. A man like Orson Latimer, with his need for love, would be married or fully occupied with an affair, and the fact that they had so nearly been lovers would have been forgotten long ago. She went back to her room, knowing that she could hand the pen into the lodge for the porter to take to Orson's room and there would be no need for her to speak to him about anything but ward matters.

She put the pen on her dressing-table, where it glinted in the light, and saw an inscription on the side. *Orson, with much love, Roma.*

Kaye looked up at the mirror and saw herself there. The long dark tresses that he had once loved and her dark eyes made more bright by the reflected blue of her robe made her recall his rough voice when he saw her with Michelle. A madonna, he had called her once with love; but now he thought that it was all a facade and he had another love who gave him inscribed pens and her devotion.

Tomorrow I shall be so involved with the work of the ward that I shall have no time for thinking of anything more. Tomorrow, she thought, as the mist of sleep dulled her tired brain, I shall face him and have no emotion left to waste on Orson Latimer. 'Vincent,' she murmured. 'If only I had loved you and let you care for me.'

She dreamed of small children who could never grow up, like those with the pituitary hormone deficiency who were coming for tests hoping that their growth could be stimulated and they would no longer suffer the snide remarks of the other children who grew tall and strong in the same environment. If she could help them, in any way, however insignificant, wasn't that enough to justify her return to Beattie's? Ben Hanley had told her of several children he had seen after treatment who rushed to show him their growth charts and boasted how they had outgrown two sizes in jeans in the past few months. When Kaye woke, she felt fresh and was smiling.

Sister March was leaving the dining-room as Sister Harcourt went up to fetch her breakfast. It was still quite early and Kaye had the feeling that March was avoiding her now that there must have been a meeting between the new sister and Orson Latimer. Even March must feel a bit awkward, knowing that Dr Hanley would have mentioned her offer to welcome the newcomer.

One or two of the other sisters made a point of saying hello and inviting Kaye for coffee in one of the ward duty rooms when she had a break. They all seemed bright and attractive and young, except for Casualty Sister and the senior theatre superintendent who had been at Beattie's for years and showed no signs of leaving to get married, spread their wings or for any other purpose. So many attractive sisters and nurses—plenty to fill idle moments for the handsome American, thought Kaye.

Michelle was walking round the main ward

hugging a huge soft toy that looked a bit like a lion but had lost its tail.

'You're up early, Michelle,' said Sister Harcourt. The child smiled, showing the gap in her teeth. She said nothing but put her hand in the one held out to her and together they went into the office. 'You are almost better,' said Kaye. 'Do you know when you can go home?' Michelle shook her head vigorously. 'Did you finish your puzzle?' She nodded. 'Well, go into the day room and find another puzzle or a book and I'll come and see you when I've written in my book.'

'No. There's a man in there.'

'A man? You mean one of the doctors? They are very nice men and like little girls.'

'This one is big.' Michelle sat on the floor in the corner and sucked her thumb.

'You can't stay there, Michelle. The floor is cold and I have work to do. Come on, I'll take you along and help you choose.' Sister called the staff nurse. 'Can you start my round and I'll come to take report from the night staff as soon as I can. Any word from Michelle's parents?'

'No, Sister. An aunt called yesterday and saw one of the doctors. She asked to see you, I believe, but you were off when she was downstairs. She said she will come in this morning.'

Kaye went with Michelle, who held on tightly to the protective hand. The door of the day room was open and on the table was the orderly chaos that is the best that can be obtained with toys of all shapes and types. Gaily-coloured boxes filled with soft toys and building bricks lay ready for use, and a pile of books sat on a low stool.

Michelle rushed to the books and pulled them over into a heap, sinking to her knees to look through them. Then she tensed and her face once more looked smaller and sad. The tall man in the white coat who was talking to the children in for tests, rose from the pre-formed plastic chair and looked at her.

'Hello,' he said in a deep warm voice, and smiled.

'It's all right,' said Kaye, as Michelle tried to bury her head in her skirt. 'It's only Dr Latimer. He works here and loves little girls.' She was torn between sympathy for the child and amusement. Of course Dr Latimer loved girls . . . of all ages. He gave her a sharp look, seeing the gentle quiver of her lips. 'Come on, Michelle. He is quite harmless, very good-tempered and is very good at jigsaw puzzles.'

One large eye peeped round but Michelle still clung tightly to the now crumpled skirt.

'It's true. Sister knows me quite well.' Orson grinned slightly. 'She also has a very good memory. I had no idea you remembered the puzzle we did.' Kaye blushed. What had made her mention that? 'Sister is very good at edges and I do the sky.'

Two eyes were now visible, filled with suspicion but at least not full of tears.

'You are Michelle?' She nodded and Sister Harcourt lowered her to the floor by the pile of books. Orson Latimer went back to the other children and Michelle ignored him, although he looked at her from time to time with the serious, caring regard that Kaye had once known. He was harder on the surface and had no time for past loves, but he was still fond of children and treated each as an individual. The bull was gentle today, backing away so that he wouldn't scare the small child who had such a bad opinion of large men.

Kaye crept away, with one last look to make sure that Michelle was engrossed and no longer thought that Dr Latimer was a threat. She took report and looked at the admissions list and then went from bed to bed to check that every small patient had been bathed and tidied before the consultant's round in half an hour.

The dull throb of young voices was normal and without tension and each bed and cot held a child responding to care. The two intravenous drips were working in copy-book style and the congenital dislocation of hip, now in plaster, gave less trouble than before Mandy came into the ward and to the theatre. Once more, Kaye marvelled at the way children adapted to hospital. Mandy was on her back with her legs in the air as if she was trying to be a television aerial, with thick white antennae, but she was also reading a book and laughing at the cartoons.

'Have the T's and A's been prepared, Nurse?'

'Yes, Sister. They have had nothing by mouth since yesterday tea-time. Night Sister managed to take away a bar of chocolate that one had hidden in his locker, left by an adoring mum in case we starve him! They've had their pre-medication and the first is due in theatre in half an hour.'

'So early? Aren't they at the end of the list any more?'

'No. Now that Dr Charumbera is helping, the surgical registrar in the ENT department does a minor list once a week and leaves the tonsils and adenoids to his house surgeon. They have only a cold mastoid this morning before they do the two from here and three dissection of tonsils in older children in Men's Surgical side ward. It does mean that ours can have all day to recover and we can keep a better watch on them than at night in a dimly lit ward. The end cubicles are quiet as most of the up patients go to the day room at the other end of the ward and leave them in peace.'

A pretty blonde girl in a white coat came into the ward carrying a small case. She smiled and said that she had come to collect blood from the first of the PHS children. Sister Harcourt took her into the day room where Dr Latimer was still talking to the children.

'Hello, Elizabeth,' he said, and looked very pleased to see her. She smiled and suggested that the two children might go to their side ward. Dr Latimer went with them and Kaye found herself wondering if the pretty medical scientist was another of the handsome doctor's conquests. Certainly they seemed very much at home in each other's company and were on first name terms. The new work with children, which included so many tests and so much scientific assessment, must throw doctors into the company of the bright and far too attractive girls who did this work.

Kaye shook off her thoughts and concentrated on the off-duty rota which still had to be made up for the next week. Pretty girls in any department were not of interest to her, even if Dr Latimer made love to each one of them. He was welcome to please himself, and so was she now. And when Tony

Smythe put his cheerful face round her door, asking for coffee, she laughed and invited him in, but warned him that there would be no coffee for anyone until the round was over. She busied herself getting notes and X-rays in order on a small trolley and was ready when Dr Ben Hanley arrived with his team of foreign students and his own registrar.

'Hello, Nurse Harcourt.' The registrar laughed. 'Oh, I *do* beg your pardon, *Sister*.'

'And you were only a house surgeon when I left. How are you, Hugh?' Kaye greeted him with a smile.

'All the better for knowing that you will be here to get me out of trouble with our Ben,' he whispered. 'He works us all into the ground.'

'I don't believe it.' Her eyes sparkled. Yet another old friend surfacing, and he was a man who had been a very good friend in the old days. 'See you later,' she said, giving him a dazzling smile.

'And we can find out where we left off.' He gave her arm a squeeze and grinned. He hadn't changed. Hugh Worth had a reputation for being all talk and no action when it came to flirting, but he was fun and had a heart of gold. A tender smile touched her lips. There were still very many memories that she wouldn't want to fade and Hugh was a part of the happy life she had found at Beattie's before the golden bull had charged into her life and wrecked it.

She knew that someone was watching her by the prickly feeling at the back of her neck. She looked up from the trolley and saw Orson Latimer looking from her to Hugh and back again. Tony Smythe patted her arm in passing and whispered, 'Coffee later,' in her ear before going over to the theatre block to see the T's and A's. It all appeared as if Kaye knew the two men very well and had a very free relationship with them.

Orson's smile was half quizzical and half sardonic, as if it was almost a relief that he found her to be as he believed, a woman with love for everyone who asked for it and no true loyalty to just one man. She turned away and the next hour or so was filled with the round, the bedside lecture and the assessment of notes and scientific findings.

Once, Kaye found Orson close behind her as she waited for Dr Hanley to leave a bedside, but this time she avoided colliding with him as she had done when he was waiting for the telephone. She remembered the pen, now safe in her pocket, and handed it to him. He looked into her eyes and she caught her breath. In the depths was sadness that she had never imagined was possible for him. He took the pen and carefully turned it between his fingers before putting it in the pocket of his white coat.

'Thank you,' he said. 'I forgot that you borrowed it.'

'I'm sorry. I discovered it last night after you had gone.'

'I'm very pleased to see it again. It means a great deal to me and I would hate to lose it.'

Kaye followed Ben Hanley to the office. So, the pen was not just valuable because it was gold-plated. Orson really cared about it and about the person who had her name engraved on it. Roma. A romantic name for a romantic woman? A woman he still loved, or he would have not attached so much importance to the pen.

CHAPTER THREE

'Is Nelson Charumbera here?'

'Oh, hello, Ercil. What do you want with our houseman?'

'Don't you worry, girl, you can have him back. I only want him to see a boy in my ward.' Sister Ercil Kingston laughed and, as usual, Kaye warmed to her and smiled, even though this morning she was not feeling her best. 'We have a boy who is big for his age but too young for a men's ward. He has earache real bad and I'm worried. They sent him up from Casualty but couldn't bleep Nelson. The boy's in his bed and feeling very sorry for himself and I need someone to see him in a hurry.'

'We are full just now,' said Sister Harcourt, frowning. 'I don't like these in-betweens being with grown men. The men spoil them and often make them feel worse than they are—it pays to make a fuss when surrounded by sympathy. Has he a history of otitis media?'

'His family have moved to this part of the country and this is his first time in hospital. His poor father had to leave him as the actual house move is being completed today and he wanted to make sure that his wife had everything she needed.'

'He's coming back?'

'Oh yes, he's very concerned. In a way, he's better helping at the farm.'

'Farm? They must live some distance away.

Have you Dr Charumbera's number?'

Kaye tried the doctors' common room and the dining-room and found the internal phone of the apartment block engaged.

'I expect the silly man has switched off his bleeper again. It happens all the time, so Tony Smythe says. I'm going over to lunch and I can pop in to the house and see if he is there. I can also make sure the phone is back on the rest and not lying there for someone to answer, forgotten and unusable.'

'Thanks, Kaye. I have to get back as we have a round due shortly. If he needs to do a paracentisis, can I borrow some instruments from you?' Ercil asked.

'Sounds as if he should be in surgical, but I know that sometimes earache is left to settle for a day or so if the drum isn't bulging badly.' Kaye went to the door. 'I'll ring you from the home if he isn't there. If not, who will you get? Can I take a message while I'm there in case it's someone not on call and not listening in?'

'I never know who to call in these cases. He isn't a small child and he isn't strictly a man and he hasn't been diagnosed as medical or surgical yet.' Ercil looked puzzled.

'Bleep Tony and ask him to look in. They will have finished in theatre by now and he can get in touch with Dr Hanley if he thinks it necessary.'

'I suppose that's best, if you can't raise Nelson. I haven't been in charge for long enough to be confident about asking some of the doctors in case I upset the firm.'

'I feel the same, and with these new teams there seems to be no one actually in charge of the whole unit all the time. We have the housemen and the consultant and we are supposed to have a registrar, but he spends more time at other units gathering data on any child likely to be helped by the growth hormone programme. I must admit that the results coming through seem to make it very worthwhile, but some of the team who are here only as observers have had to be called in to help out sometimes,' Kaye grumbled.

'The gorgeous Orson?'

'Not if I can avoid it,' said Kaye sharply and left the smile to fade on Ercil's pleasant face. She shrugged and went back to her own ward, and Kaye Harcourt went quickly across to the home, hoping that this time there would be no need to call on Dr Orson Latimer for help. She slackened her pace. What was there for her to worry about? If she had to contact him, it would be for Ercil and the medical ward and she need only give a brief message.

The hall was deserted and, as she suspected, someone had failed to put back the arm of the telephone receiver after use. She replaced it and decided to write a note and leave it by the phone. If something urgent was needed, this could be a serious lapse.

She went up to the room where Nelson Charumbera lived and tapped on the door. He opened it and she saw that he had a heavy cold. He was swathed in a thick dressing-gown, although the room was stifling, and Kaye backed away instinctively from the heat and the risk of infection.

'I can see that you are in no fit state to be on the wards,' she said. 'Who is standing in for you?'

'Didn't you get my message, Sister?' His voice was a painful croak and his eyes looked heavy and watering.

'Message? No, I was asked by Ercil Kingston to find you as there has been an emergency admission on her ward—a child with query otitis media. She tried to bleep you but no one could find you. I tried the dining-room and common room . . .' she stopped. 'You really did send a message?'

He nodded and began to cough. 'She offered to tell you,' he said. 'She must have told *someone*.'

'Not me, for sure,' said Kaye firmly. 'Who was it? One of my nurses? I'll have her guts for garters. This isn't good enough. What if something urgent required your attention?'

'What indeed, Sister Kaye.' The huge brown eyes looked puzzled. 'I thought she was so kind, so friendly. She even brought me these things and said I was to stay in bed. I told her I'd things to do but she said there were plenty of doctors doing nothing who would help out if she asked, and that you would organise everything once she gave you the message.'

Kaye glanced beyond him to the table and saw a pretty tray arranged with a few small flowers in a tiny vase and some delicious looking sandwiches with a vacuum flask of a hot drink. It must have taken quite a time to do and been planned, so how could whoever did this have forgotten the one vital thing, to give the sister in charge of the children's ward the message that the houseman was ill? She bit her lip. 'You haven't told me who it was, Doctor.'

'Why, Sister March, of course. She said what

good friends you were and she'd be seeing you in any case.'

'Sister March is . . . has made a mistake. I have not seen her this morning. I have been very busy with two of the children and I shall ask all the staff if they took any message at all, but I'm pretty certain that none was given.' He looked at her pale face and flashing eyes. 'In future, if Sister March offers to help me, please ignore it. With her on the staff, who needs enemies?'

Kaye tried to smile. 'I'm sorry to sound off like this, but she really does not like me and we have nothing in common.' She thought rapidly. 'I'm not being up-tight. Think what could have happened. The registrar is over at Great Ormond Street today, Tony Smythe was in theatre and might still be there and you are sick. Dr Hanley is looking at private cases in a hospital a few miles away and no other doctor has been alerted.'

'I'll have to get dressed,' he said. 'Someone must see that boy and do something soon if he's acute.'

'You can't. You would do more harm than good in the state you're in. Who is there available with enough seniority to make a decision?'

'Thought you'd never ask.' Kaye Harcourt started and turned.

'You?' She stared at Dr Orson Latimer, who lounged against the doorpost of the room adjoining. He was dressed in leisure clothes and her heart contracted painfully. He had always looked good in tight jeans and sweat shirt and today the dark blue shirt made his hair seem extra bright and his eyes deep and wonderfully sensual.

'You look terrible,' he said to the doctor. 'Get your head down and I'll cope.'

'But you are not on the regular staff,' Kaye protested.

'I may not be now, but you know my work and I am a Beatties man.' His smile mocked her. 'And I don't think I have to apply to a ward sister for a job here. I know Ben Hanley would approve, even if you find my presence on your ward distasteful.' He turned away. 'I'll be on the ward in ten minutes. Men's Medical, you mentioned? Good. I shall have no need to bother you, Sister.'

He had heard it all. He must have heard it if he knew the child was on Medical. He must have heard all that she had said about Sister March and that might account for his sarcasm. Kaye recalled the time before she left the hospital to do her midwifery. March had made a dead set at him as soon as the first cracks of suspicion had eroded the relationship between the American and the dark-haired nurse, offering him sympathy and comfort and adding fire on fire with soft hints of Kaye Harcourt's infidelity. Surely, after this time, she had either gained what she wanted from him or given up the attempt to make him love her? Kaye felt a chill of apprehension. Sister March was a very devious and dangerous person who had lost none of her dislike for the new sister.

'I'll tell Sister Kingston,' she said.

'No need. I shall be there.'

'I promised,' she said coldly. 'And I give messages when I say I will.'

'And keep promises?' The slight sneer showed that he had forgotten nothing and still believed that she had been unfaithful all that time ago.

Kaye walked away to the house phone and rang Men's Medical. 'Dr Orson Latimer will be with you in a few minutes,' she told Ercil Kingston. 'Nelson has a very bad cold or the flu and can't be here, but Dr Latimer volunteered to help out.'

She went down for her belated lunch and hurried through the main course, deciding to have coffee back on the ward if she had the time. She saw Sister March leave the dining-room and couldn't bear to speak to her in case she said something very rude and demeaning. The least said the better, but it was time to make sure that anyone of importance knew that Sister Kaye Harcourt preferred to receive her messages through the usual channels of ward telephones and staff on duty.

As she went back to the ward she heard crying and Nurse Benson met her, looking anxious. 'What is it, Nurse?'

'It's Michelle. She is having hysterics and her rash is coming back. Her face is puffed up and her arm is very oedematous.'

'How bad? Is it as bad as when she was admitted?' Kaye recalled the notes that showed clearly the amount of swelling by measurement of the child's arms round the wrists and round the upper arm where the tissues had become water-logged— the allergic reaction to stress had made histamine flow as if she had been stung by several very fierce bees.

'It isn't serious yet, Sister, but it ties up with hysteria.'

'What happened? Something must have caused it.'

They reached the door of the side ward but Sister Harcourt wanted details before talking in front of Michelle. 'Her father came to see her and she just burst into tears and ran into the sluice to hide,' Nurse Benson explained.

'I see. Was her mother there too?'

'She waited in the corridor as he said he wanted to see Michelle alone.'

'You didn't leave them alone?' Nurse Benson shook her head. 'Well, we'll see what is to be done.'

'Michelle's aunt is here now, Sister. She seems worried and wouldn't come up to the ward when the parents were here. I asked the parents to wait in the office and sent the aunt in with the junior nurse to see Michelle.'

The crying had stopped and a rather overweight woman was bending over the child, speaking softly. She looked up as if afraid and then smiled. 'I tried to see you before, Sister,' she said. 'I'm Mrs Clark and Michelle's mother is my sister.'

Michelle was cuddled up to the woman now and her face was swollen with tears and the onset of the giant urticaria.

'She seems happy with you,' said Kaye Harcourt, hoping to gain her confidence.

'Yes, she's a nice little thing.' Mrs Clark smoothed the damp hair from the swollen face and gave Michelle a quick hug. 'I want to take her home with me. I can't say anything to upset my sister and her husband, but Michelle doesn't fit in there and never will.'

'They came to see her today.' Sister Harcourt pointed towards the office. She didn't tell Michelle where her parents were waiting but the aunt understood and frowned. 'I believe that it upset Michelle. The lady from the social services gave me a report and, personally, I'd welcome you taking control if it can be arranged.'

'My sister rang me and asked me to come, but *he* isn't what you might call a man you can reason with.'

'This is difficult. I am in no position to demand anything and as yet there has been no proven cause for the child to leave home.' Mrs Clark tossed her head. 'But Michelle is obviously relaxed with you, Mrs Clark,' Kaye said quickly. 'I'll ring down to the social worker and perhaps you could all see her.'

The door opened and she was aware of someone coming into the room, but she continued to write the note she wanted to send down to the social worker, detailing the allergic condition brought on whenever Michelle saw her father.

'For crying out . . . What gives with her?' Orson Latimer whispered. He stood by the door and didn't venture closer as Michelle took one look at him and clung to her aunt again.

'Could we discuss this outside, Dr Latimer? Michelle just doesn't care for huge men who seem to threaten her.'

He grinned. 'You been brainwashing her about me?'

'Of course not,' Kaye said, with a trace of irritation. 'Her father is big and blonde and a bit rough and any man remotely resembling him gives her a rash.'

'So I'm big and blonde and a bit rough, did you say?'

'You know what I mean.' She stood tall and eyed him with coolness that hid her inner turmoil. 'The parents are in my office and the aunt, who is very fond of Michelle, wants to take her home with her. I'm going to ring down to the social worker and see if she can sort this out. In a way it's not a bad thing for the rash to come back now. It does prove a link between her condition and something that happens at home.'

He was watching her, his eyes very blue and solemn and his body loose and easy against the wall. Why can some men look completely elegant and macho even standing against a wall with hands thrust deep into the pockets of a creased white coat? She tried to look away, but her eyes wanted to regard him while he answered and her heart wanted to ask if he was happy. The neck of the coat was turned in as if he had pulled it on as he strode along the corridor and had no idea how he looked. She wanted to turn back the collar and smooth the rever into neatness. Above all, she wondered how it would be if he touched her.

'I'll see him if you like.'

'I don't know; I thought the social worker and then possibly Dr Hanley,' she said cautiously. If two large men met and one was belligerently on guard because he thought people might accuse him of beating his child, it was uncertain what might happen.

'Sometimes a woman can handle these situations better,' she said.

Orson looked at her with what might in the past have passed for tenderness and an affectionate amusement, but which she now thought must be derision. 'One small madonna instead of a bull? You might be right.'

He ran his hand through his hair, brushing the situation and the ward sister from his mind. 'I came to tell you about the boy in Men's Med. He's acute and should be done now. Ercil will ring through in about ten minutes and bring him along. Can I have a tray ready?'

'You mean to do it here?'

'You object?' His voice took a hard note.

'No, I can have everything ready, but we haven't a bed.'

'He'll go back the way he came but I'd rather do it here. There is no need to alert theatre for something as small as this, but I don't want him upset by taking him to Casualty theatre.'

Orson pulled on the tubes of the stethoscope that hung from his neck until Kaye thought it might snap. 'You know what it's like down there if an accident comes in,' he said.

For a full minute they looked at each other, remembering a night when they had worked for three hours on one accident case, too ill to move further to the major theatre block and too messy to take to a ward, until they had him stitched and cleaned and transfused. Orson smiled wryly. 'You do remember.'

She nodded. It was cruel of him to pluck at her emotions and to remind her of that night, the work in utter harmony, the exhaustion after it was over and the sweetness of their tired kisses, too tired for passion but full of a deep and wonderful togetherness.

'I'll have a tray ready in the clinical room and we

can close the inner door so that you are not disturbed and the children in the ward will not be affected.' She left him and asked Nurse Benson to lay up a tray for myringotomy and to have plenty of dressings ready, together with a small suction apparatus.

The social worker was relieved to know that all the people most concerned with the future of Michelle were in one place at the same time. She said she'd drop all her other work and come right away and Sister Harcourt breathed a sigh of relief. It was too easy to become involved in the work of other departments and very difficult to refuse to help when her natural sympathy and compassion urged to her take charge and to put matters over which she had no official control to right. She smiled, wondering if it might be easier to face one big man with a foul temper and a chip on his shoulder than to meet another big man with skilled hands and a sensual mouth who had once loved her.

Nurse Benson flicked the towel over the tray on one of the glass-topped trolleys and then put a pack of bandages and strapping on the lower shelf with various tinctures and a drop bottle of spirit in a white dish.

'Tell me what you have on the tray, Nurse?'

'A pack of sterile swabs, a galley-pot of mercurochrome to clean up the surrounding area and swab holders. I put three sizes of aural speculae as we don't know the size of the ear and the headlamp is on the bottom of the trolley with a reflector if that's what Dr Orson prefers. There are two long-handled angled forceps so that he can see the ear drum and not have his view obscured by his own hand. A sterile pad and dressing and a choice of myringotomes. You asked me at the right time, Sister,' Nurse Benson laughed. 'I had to look it up last week to tell some of the juniors when we had another case in and they had never heard of slitting the ear drum to let out infected fluid and relieve the tension.'

'Very good. It's amazing how much we learn when we have to teach other people. I spent my first few months as senior staff nurse re-learning all the basic treatments I thought I remembered and found I knew them only in outline.'

Kaye glanced at her watch and went to see if the trolley carrying the boy was in sight. 'No need to wait, Nurse. I'll see to this. There is no need to scrub as Dr Latimer will do it alone. I'll just stay to keep . . . What is his name? Ah, yes, to keep Colin still and calm if possible. I'd better have a gown in case I get discharge over my uniform.'

A familiar form stood by the sink and looked at the tray on which Nurse Benson had put a pack of large-sized sterile rubber gloves and a sterile gown and mask ready for him. The door swung open silently and Ercil and a nurse pushed the trolley into the clinical room.

'Sorry about this, girl, but I think he's right. Our clinical room is like Piccadilly Circus with nosey patients trying to see what goes on in there.' Ercil looked down at the pale face on the pillow. 'He should be with you, Kaye, but I suppose he's lucky to be admitted with the full wards we have just now.'

Kaye Harcourt smiled down at the boy and put

the brake on the trolley, as it was to serve as the operating table. Purposely she let him get used to her without a mask before tying it on casually and putting gentle hands on his shoulders.

'It will be so much more comfortable in a little while,' she said, and he smiled faintly.

'Sister? Can you tie my gown?' She left the boy and was faced with the broad back of the doctor, standing with the white gown on his arms but trailing tie tapes behind him. Kaye smiled. It was always this way in theatre. The random selection of gowns, folded in the sterile drums, often matched badly with the people wearing them. She usually managed to get one far too long over which she tripped unless it was tied firmly and bunched up round her waist, and men like Orson Latimer picked gowns that would be perfect on her but had to be tied at the ends of the tapes when they wore them. In theory, one drum contained large gowns and one small, but faced with far more of one size than the other and told to fill the drums and not to waste valuable space, the nurse packing them often put in any that were back from the laundry, and it was impossible to label them in sizes.

Kaye tied the top tape and he grunted that it was tight. He braced his back impatiently and snapped it off from the gown, making it impossible to tie. She produced a safety-pin and made the join, slackening the tie as much as possible. The other tapes just met and Orson picked up the swab soaked in the red antiseptic paint. Kaye Harcourt stood by the boy, her hand turning his head on the pillows so that the affected ear was uppermost. He closed his eyes as if dizzy—and he might well have been as the tense middle ear made pressure on the organ of balance in the inner ear.

Orson nodded and gently inserted the hollow cone of metal through which he could see inside the ear. It was cold and the boy winced but Kaye was reassuring. The clear beam of light from the head-lamp showed the tense tympanic membrane or eardrum, with fine blood-vessels over the surface of the surrounding tissues. With a small swab of cotton wool on the end of the forceps, he gently cleaned away traces of ear wax and discharge and then took the tiny knife on the angled handle. Kaye braced herself to hold the boy firmly if necessary.

A quick contact of sharp blade on the tense drum was all that was required. It was over in a second and the discharge flowed from the clean cut easily. This would drain and become clear, the incision would heal without a scar and the boy should suffer no complications.

Kaye Harcourt knew that if this had been neg-lected and the eardrum had burst under pressure, the badly scarred tympanus might mar hearing and it was possible that unreleased fluid might take infection down to the inner ear and to the mastoid process, giving rise to much more acute suffering and risk to hearing and general health.

'Fine, just fine.' The warm voice was deep and pleased. 'Just another swab, I think, and we are there.'

He swabbed away the profuse discharge and inserted spirit drops to dry the lining of the ear and to mop up the residual exudate. Kaye placed a thick pad of cotton wool and gauze over the ear and held the boy's head while the doctor bandaged it in position.

'One thing I can do is to put on a neat bandage, and I defy anyone to say it will slip off in the night.' Colin grinned. 'You can go home tomorrow but come back to have another dressing when Dr Charumbera says he's ready to see you. I suppose he will be better in a day or so, Sister?'

'I hope so.'

Orson raised one eyebrow and she blushed.

'I mean, for his sake,' she said.

'Well, that sure is a relief,' he said in a drawl that was usually missing from his crisp speech, acting the deep South as he had done so long ago when he wanted to tease her. 'I began to think I wasn't wanted around here.'

'Whatever gave you that idea?' she said sweetly. 'I heard that you were party boy last night with everyone queuing up for your company.'

'Not everyone. I had a cold patch on one side.'

'Don't,' she whispered. He was cruel. How could he be so cruel?

It was what he said in the old days when she left him to get a drink, go to the Ladies or was called away on duty. When she came back he would draw her close beside him and say just that . . . 'Come back, honey, you left a cold patch.'

She called the junior nurse to ring the ward sister and to go back with Colin when they were ready, then pushed the used trolley towards the sink. Orson was pulling at his gown, trying to reach the tapes.

'Let me,' she said, and found that one lower tape was in a knot and the safety-pin that she had used was pulled into the cotton material of the gown. He pulled against her. 'Hold still,' she said. 'I wonder just how many gowns you've ruined? And how many irate theatre sisters remember you leaving a trail of disaster behind you?'

She released him and took the mangled garment to the bin.

'And you never got caught up in anything you couldn't handle, did you?'

She turned away, her face glowing, but she knew that she didn't show her blushes. They went deeper and she had no release of soft infused pink cheeks and a feminine withdrawal. She reached up to untie the top tape of her gown and to her dismay it was in a tight knot. Kaye tugged and hoped that Dr Latimer would leave before he saw her predicament, but he lounged against the sink, grinning. 'Want some help?' he said, but made no move to go to her.

'I can manage. Shouldn't you be checking the PHS kids?' she said desperately.

'Nope! They are fine. All done, and I have time for coffee or a delicious cup of Beattie's tea and a cookie.'

She fiddled with the next tape and it gave. Encouraged, she undid the rest but the top one resisted every effort and grew tighter each time she tugged.

'Naughty!' he said, with an infuriating calm. 'I thought that I was the only bull in a china shop around here. You really should watch what you are doing with hospital property, Sister.' She stood defeated, knowing that it was unlikely that one of the nurses would come to rescue her unless she appeared trailing her gown in the ward.

Orson came to her and his fingers fiddled with the knot as if it was a delicate surgical manoeuvre. He stopped and his hands were on her shoulders, turning her towards him. He slid the loose white gown from her and undid the tape on her cap, lifting the mask and throwing them both to the ground. She knew that her hair was coming unpinned and was filled with a delicious panic, long forgotten, long remembered. She felt his lips on her cheek and closed her eyes, unable to breathe, then found that she was standing alone and he was at the sink vigorously scrubbing away all signs of the brief procedure, all contact with the clinical room, the patient and her. Kaye put a hand to her still immaculate hair and pushed one pin in more firmly. Bending, she picked up his cap and mask and her own protective clothing, crumpled relics that could be tossed in the soiled bin and forgotten.

Her own crisp cap seemed good now that it was back in place. It was a sign of her position, a barrier of rank between staff and patients when necessary and an almost virginal denial of sex.

She unlocked the ward door and went back to her office. One of the administrative nursing officers was coming to the ward. 'Everything all right, Sister?'

'Yes, everything is fine, Miss Maby.' Kaye looked surprised, for Miss Maby had the reputation of only appearing when some crisis threatened. The woman hesitated.

'Was there anything you wanted to know?' Kaye smiled. 'Ah, I expect you are interested in the new projects, Miss Maby. They are coming on very well and we seem to have more and more people wanting to see what the team is doing.'

'I'm sure you are busy, Sister.' Miss Maby seemed uncertain of something. 'Or were you looking for someone when you saw me coming? One of the doctors, perhaps?'

'No, they have done their rounds and the team are up to date with the charts and graphs. You couldn't have come at a better time if you want to do a round. We have just finished a small myringotomy and Dr Latimer has written up some drugs. We are well up to schedule, even with the extra work,' Kaye said cheerfully. 'It is such a happy ward most of the time.'

'So I see, Sister.' Two children were playing angelically in the day room and three were watching television. In the ward the curtains were back from most cubicles and a game of I Spy was the only noisy corner.

'Who did the rounds?' Miss Maby asked. 'Dr Hanley is away and so is Dr Smythe, I believe. I suppose Dr Charumbera saw them.' Her tone was too casual.

Does she think that I have let the day go on with no doctor seeing the patients? Kaye wondered. Suddenly, she knew that the nursing officer had been told that there was no doctor on the ward and that Sister Harcourt had let things slide without supervision.

'Dr Charumbera? Oh, no, he's not well enough to work. He turned over his work to Dr Latimer who knows Beattie's so well, Miss Maby. He has been working very hard here and I have been glad of his support.'

So March had told no one about Nelson being ill. She had told no one until she saw the administrative staff and told them that Sister Harcourt needing checking because she might be getting ideas above her status. And if I hadn't known about Nelson, I could have gone on thinking he was delayed and not knowing that he wasn't coming, Kaye realised. I could have gone off duty and left the slightly oozing tonsil case from yesterday's surgery still at risk, without medical supervision. She felt cold.

Orson Latimer came out from behind the curtains of a cubicle, thrusting them in all directions in his normal way. 'I'll make a few notes in your office, if I may, Sister. The desk along the corridor is too noisy. Now, is there anything more you want from me? I shall see Charumbera in about half an hour, take him these notes and maybe catch his cold.'

He gave Miss Maby a devastating smile. 'Your new Sister is a complete slave driver. She doesn't miss a thing. I shall escape while I may, but remember, I am available until your truant medics show up.' He laughed and cast his gaze heavenwards. 'And I thought I was coming here for some peace and quiet.'

Miss Maby blushed. 'Well, I don't see the need to do a complete round, Sister. I congratulate you on the atmosphere of the ward.' She walked slowly away.

'Going now,' said Orson briskly. 'But of course, I shall alert Tony Smythe and he can take over from me this evening.' He was watching the receding back of the woman from Admin. 'You had a slight mix-up today,' he said slowly. 'It's hard to think that anyone in authority here could fail to pass on such an important message.'

Kaye stiffened. He didn't trust her and thought that Brenda March had given her the message. 'A lot of things are hard to believe, Dr Latimer,' she said. 'I can only know what I believe and what really happened.'

'Yes.' He saw Nurse Benson coming out of the ward kitchen. 'I hope you were putting on the kettle,' he said. She laughed and blushed. 'Any of those very good cookies you gave me yesterday, Nurse?'

Nurse Benson shot an agonised glance at her superior. 'You ate them all,' she said. 'I'm sorry, Sister, but they said they were too late for coffee in the common room.'

'It's all right, Nurse. I know how difficult some of the doctors can be,' Kaye said demurely. 'Today Dr Latimer has earned his coffee. Could you send some along to the office as soon as possible?'

Kaye went into her office and unlocked the drug cupboard. 'While you wait, perhaps you could check the dangerous drugs with me, Doctor. The list is very creased and I want to start from scratch and make sure we have only those drugs that are used as routine here in the one compartment and the controlled ones in the inner locked section. I found some chloral hydrate here where anyone could take it if they had the key of the outer door.'

'My pleasure,' Orson said formally. He watched her wipe the glass shelves as she took the bottles and phials down for checking, returning everything in an orderly way that made the contents easy to see. Her neat writing filled the cards that would now be stuck to the inner door to show what stocks were present, and as the coffee came in, carried by the junior nurse who fluttered her eyelashes at the handsome American, they finished the job. The faint smell of methylated spirit used to clean the glass faded as the door was locked.

Kaye Harcourt poured coffee and handed him a cup, pushing over the tin of biscuits that she had brought for her own use in the ward. He opened the lid and she wished that she had offered him the plain digestive biscuits left over from the ward tea-time. He picked out a chocolate layer with orange cream and licked the edge like a small boy tasting a treat. She didn't know whether to laugh or cry.

I shall have to be very careful, she decided. Everywhere I go in this place holds some memory of him, and everything I do seems to trigger off something we shared. I might have known better than to offer him his favourite biscuits, but surely after two years he should have forgotten that he liked English biscuits or at least have developed more sophisticated tastes . . .

She sipped her coffee, silently cursing the fact that it was very hot and, if she was to finish it, she must stay in the office with the man who filled the small space with his physical presence, his male dominance and his utter refusal to be ignored.

'More coffee?' she said, knowing that he was not ready but having to say something to make him look away from her.

'Not yet.' He took another biscuit. 'My favourite. Do you know what I missed most when I went back home?'

'No,' she said.

'I missed these and a lot of things that went with them.' He regarded her without expression. 'Things like coffee simmering for hours in a steriliser and cold tea after a difficult case late at night.' He drank some more coffee. 'This is good and I'm real honoured, Sister. This is coffee that was only for the privileged in the old days.'

Kaye looked deep into her cup and nodded. Only two more sips and she might be able to escape. 'But someone remembered the biscuits. When Brenda March came over to the States, she dropped in to see me, bearing gifts.' Kaye looked up, startled. 'Funny thing about food. It never tastes the same away from its roots.'

'But you ate them.'

'No, I gave them to the kids, who adored them and clamoured for more.'

'I have to go,' she said. 'I must look in on the tonsillectomy from yesterday before I go off duty and I'll bleep Tony to see if he is available.'

'He's coming now. I rang through. Have some more coffee.'

'No, thank you. You said you had notes to write. Feel free to use the office and ask for anything you need,' she said. 'I'll talk to Nurse Benson and she can take over before I go.'

He rose from the swivel chair and faced her and her heart beat fast and painfully. 'You'll be here tomorrow?'

'Oh yes. I'm not taking a day off this week. I want to get really organised, so I shall take a half-day and make up the rest when I want to go away.' She smiled. 'There's a lot to learn and a lot to do.' She

could hear footsteps and thought it must be Tony
returning. She tugged at the side of her dress as if it
needed straightening and then looked up at him.
'Thank you for putting the record straight with Miss
Maby and for all your help today.'

'Don't thank me, Sister. It was only fair. After
all, no one could ever fault you for your nursing
ability.

She turned away and bumped into Tony Smythe
as she left the office.

'I'm sorry,' she said. 'Nice to have you back,
Tony. Excuse me. I must speak to Nurse Benson.'

As she escaped, she recalled the look that Orson
Latimer had in his eyes. He knew her to be good at
her work, dedicated and honest in anything to do
with her ward or her profession, but that was all.
Any hint of the love he had once vowed was for
ever had crumbled as the biscuit she found was still
in crumbs in her hand.

CHAPTER FOUR

'I THINK you have an admirer,' said Ercil Kingston. 'Colin went home two days ago and obviously told them all about us.' She laughed. 'He wasn't in here for long and was in pain most of the time, but he told his father that we were kind and beautiful and everything!'

'I like my admirers to be ten years of age,' Kaye Harcourt smiled. 'Tell him to come and say hello when he's in for a check; but of course, he might not come back. Didn't you say they had moved to a farm in Surrey? The local GP can do anything necessary and all he needs is good food, lots of fresh air and a bit of spoiling.'

'His father rang through just now and asked what perfume you used.'

'Oh, no! Not again.' Kaye had vivid memories of ex-patients who tried to show their gratitude in the most extravagant ways. Once she had been sent a sheaf of lovely flowers with an absurd note attached and Orson had seen it in her room. His comments had been unprintable and his jealous annoyance had lasted for more than a week, until he cooled off and admitted that he had suffered from women who vowed they had fallen in love with him.

'I told him that gifts of that nature were not encouraged and that we had done very little for his son.' Ercil sighed. 'Colin's mother is rather sweet and she left me some chocolates, which is fine, but

Mr Rocco seems to be trying to extend his links with us more than I like. It's all right if they give sweets or cakes that the whole staff can share, but I don't like gifts that are obviously expensive and very personal.'

'Just tell him I'm allergic to scent.'

'Too late. Young Colin said you smelled nice, but I think he got the message. I saw him twice in the ward and he's a very nice guy but a bit volatile. I think he is half Spanish or South American and very emotional. Colin is an only son and his father was very worried about him. He said he'd leave the perfume but that we must all go to his house-warming when they have the farmhouse finished.'

'That might be fine. Colin is no longer a patient and if he includes all the staff who helped, it does dilute the gratitude a bit.' Kaye laughed. 'I remember once I was invited to a hunt ball because a private patient came in late one night after a riding accident. His thigh was broken and he was in deep shock at first, so they brought him straight to theatre, complete with all his gear.'

She chuckled. 'I had to cut away his riding breeches after he was anaesthetised and get his leg prepared as we couldn't move him enough to re-move the tight clothing. At the ball, he danced with me and asked where I came into the picture as he couldn't recall seeing me at the hospital.'

'Did he think you were gatecrashing?'

'No, he knew I was with the hospital party and they certainly made us very welcome. When he asked me, the music stopped and there was one of those awful silences when every word that you had been fighting to make heard over the music and chatter comes through loud and clear. I was the one, I said, who cut you out of your breeches! Poor lamb, he was so embarrassed. Everyone tittered and he went quite red. Then he laughed and said very gallantly that if he had to have his trousers removed by a beautiful lady, he couldn't have chosen better!'

'At least this was only a myringotomy, and the father wasn't even there,' said Ercil.

'I'm going to listen to music tonight. Vincent is taking me to a concert at the Barbican and we are having dinner first. Half-days are rather nice. It gives me time to get up to the West End and to look around the shops before we have an early dinner at leisure and enjoy being pampered.'

'Lucky you. My man is so tied up with work that we never seem to get together unless we have a weekend off. That's not due for another two weeks, so if Mr Rocco asks me to his house-warming I think I shall go, if I can persuade you to come too.'

'Might be fun,' said Kaye. 'In which case we can take a bottle of wine or some *petits fours* and make the balance even. But I'd better go and put on something ravishing and get started if I'm to go to Harrods now.'

'Why don't you marry the guy?'

'It wouldn't work, at least not yet. I think that Vincent would like it but he knows how I feel. Besides, he is quite comfortable as he is and he isn't made for marriage.'

Ercil yawned. 'A dull day.' She stretched. 'And when it is a dull day on Men's Med, you have to believe that it *is* a dull day.' She smiled. 'Have a nice day.' She stopped at the door. 'What is the concert? There were some free tickets lying about this morning but I'm not sure if they were for the same one. I haven't heard of any celebrities in the private wing lately who were likely to scatter tickets among the staff.'

'Have the tickets all gone?'

'I don't know. Claud had them in the lodge.' Ercil laughed. 'They can really trust Claud to find a good home for them. Anyone would think he was giving the concert, but at least we know the staff will get them as he hates music unless it is straight from old music halls.'

'If it's the same one, I'd like to know. It would save Vincent a journey out here if I could get a lift. He insists on bringing me back unless I have someone with me. It isn't necessary. The tube to the Oval and then a taxi works fine, and the weather is good.'

Half an hour later, Kaye emerged from her room fresh and changed and determined to forget work and any of the staff at Beattie's who had irritated her or hurt her during her first week at the hospital. A trip out into the normal world might be good for her, she decided, and Vincent was good to be with when she was tired or miserable. But I'm not tired, not miserable, she thought. There was just a dull ache lurking somewhere inside that refused to go away and yet had no direct cause.

She put a light cardigan of pale yellow round her shoulders and hoped that it would be warm enough if she was out late, but the sun was bright and the weather forecast good, so she decided that she could manage with only a light covering over her silky pale green dress. Her copper-coloured sandals had high heels and the sleek tights gave her the kind of underpinnings that could have fitted a film star.

She bit her lip. It would all be wasted on Vincent, who thought she looked good in anything from shabby sweat shirts and jeans to full evening dress and probably wouldn't remember what she had worn on the last occasion they went out together. He was so undemanding. So unlike one man in her life.

'You look good enough to eat,' called Tony Smythe. 'Come to the concert with me tonight.'

'I'm booked,' she said, and hurried on, but when she got nearly to the gate she wished she had stopped to ask for more details. She walked back to the lodge where Claud, the hospital porter, sat in his cubby-hole and watched the life and drama of The Princess Beatrice Hospital flow by each day.

'Hello, Claud. Have you given away all the tickets?'

'Sister Harcourt.' He beamed at her, taking note of everything about her, including the fact that she wore no ring on the ring finger of her left hand. 'It's good to see you again. All the best come back here after they've sampled some of the places they go to after training.' He sniffed. 'They come back or get married, or both. I suppose you only came until you get hitched.'

'Dear old Claud,' she said lightly. 'How well you know us all.' She smiled sweetly. 'The tickets? Which concert is it?'

'They've all gone. If I'd known, I'd have saved you a couple. First in the queue, you'd have been.'

'I only want to know which one it is in case there

is a nurse or sister who can share a taxi with me on the way back.'

He reached down into the dark depths of his desk and produced a small poster. 'Chopping,' he said. 'All that pianner music gets on my wick.'

'Oh, good. It's the same one. Any idea who is going?'

'Well, now, let me see. There's Nurse Bright who had two tickets for her and her boyfriend, and a nurse came down from one of the wards for a couple for the sister up there. I don't know which one.' He looked annoyed, as if he had been done out of his right to know everything about everyone.

'What about Dr Smythe? He called out that he might be going.'

'You don't want a lift in that car of his, Sister. A right mess it is and not your sort at all.'

'I'll remember that, Claud. I think I saw it yesterday and I'm inclined to agree that it isn't the best form of travel for a girl in a light summer dress.' She had seen the open sports car steaming gently by the entrance and thought it looked fun—if the passenger was dressed in two sweaters and a tight scarf over her head.

'Not like one car here, Sister.' Claud looked crafty. 'But you know that one, don't you? Dr Latimer always did like comfort and those big American jobs are pure luxury.'

'I have no idea what car Dr Latimer drives and American cars are much too soft in the suspension to suit me. They make me sick,' she added with feeling.

Claud watched her go down to the bus stop and wondered what really had happened all that time ago. Sister March was full of veiled hints but she never really said anything. Didn't know if he could believe her, anyway, he thought. But any man who jilted a lovely girl like Sister Harcourt wanted his head read.

Kaye waited in the warm sunshine and as the bus stopped and she climbed on to the rear platform, she saw an immense yellow American car pull out of the main drive. The man at the wheel had warm golden hair that shone like a cob of corn in a field of the same yellow. By his side sat a woman with brown hair and Kaye glimpsed a silk print dress similar to one she had seen in a West End salon. Kaye sank back on the dusty seat and had to cling to the one in front as the bus lurched forward.

The smooth car drew alongside and paused to let the bus gain speed and its position on the road. The passenger was beautiful, with wide green eyes, a tip-tilted nose and the careless charm of a girl on the brink of womanhood. The car was beside the bus now, waiting for a gap in the traffic, and the man at the wheel glanced up and saw Kaye Harcourt framed in the gentle colours that suited her so well. His blue eyes glowed with reluctant admiration, then he turned to the girl and laughed. She looked up and Kaye knew that they were talking about her as the car surged forward and was lost in the line of traffic ahead.

The bus seemed to take ages and it smelled of stale tobacco, even though the notice said clearly that smoking was allowed only on the top deck. But at last Kaye alighted at Victoria and looked around for the bus stop to take her to the shops she planned to visit. A long line of people waited and time was passing, leaving her with less opportunity for leisurely strolling. She sighed. The girl in the car was already in town or wherever she wanted to be. Orson would take her to the door, even if it was inconvenient. She tried to blot out the picture of the girl and the easy warmth she shared with the man who was giving her a lift. Was he picking her up by appointment, or was he firmly involved with her?

She saw her bus approaching and held out her hand. At that moment a huge American car came from the direction of the long distance and airport coach station and passed the bus, weaving in and out of the traffic with skill and speed.

He must be seeing the girl on to a coach or making sure she got to the airport, Kaye thought. Something about her had labelled the girl as American. She had come to visit Orson . . . and that would account for his absence from the ward during the past few days. The night staff said that he checked up on notes and saw his patients about midnight but no one on day duty had seen him.

The afternoon faded although the sun shone, and Kaye wondered if she had been over-working. Why should she feel heavy and depressed when she was free to enjoy the delights of London, had a good evening planned and knew she looked lovely?

She stopped for a cool drink in a side-road café and convinced herself that the sudden warm weather was responsible for her lassitude. Birds sang in the dusty plane trees and she longed for the country, as she had done when she and Orson had spent days walking the muddy hillsides of Box Hill and the Downs.

She swallowed hard. It's no use, I shall have to leave, she decided. Every time I round a corner, I hold my breath in case he is there. Each time a man comes to the ward wearing a white coat, my heart does somersaults—and I can never settle down in any hospital where he is working. It was stupid to expect memories to fade when the two people concerned were back in the same place again, and she was suffering. Oh, God, how much more? she thought bitterly. Why did he come back?

Vincent was waiting patiently for her in the foyer of the Barbican and kissed her cheek, smiling down at her as if she was just what he wanted for his birthday. She smiled gratefully. Dear man. He was so much a part of her life and yet could share nothing that really mattered. She put a hand on his arm, wanting human contact, and he led her into the bar where he had ordered drinks before the concert and more for the interval. They sat on the low seats and talked about anything and yet nothing; it was soothing not to have to make an effort to amuse or to entertain. Vincent was full of the details of his new office and urged her to come to see it when she could find the time.

Kaye looked about her at the mixed crowd and wondered if the idea of casual dress really did much to help the atmosphere of a prestigious place like a major concert hall. The foyer was filling up with foreign visitors disgorged from many coaches and descending on the bar with the precision and force of an army of occupation. One woman was dressed in furs and looked very hot but determined to impress, and others had such casual clothes that they could have just come from a beach.

'I think there may be people from Beattie's here. There were several complimentary tickets on offer and we have a very thriving music club, so I'm sure they weren't wasted,' Kaye said.

'That would account for it.' Vincent looked back into a crush of people. 'I thought I saw one of your sisters over there.'

'Oh, who was it? I didn't think you knew many of the ones there now. Don't tell me that Sister Bates likes Chopin!'

'I remember her. No, this was the blonde who was there before you left. Did she leave too, or has she stayed on? She looks far too go-ahead to remain in one place for long.'

'Sister March?'

'Really a sister? I called her Sister, but I recall that she was a staff nurse like you at the time. Shall I get her a drink if I can find her?'

'No.'

Vincent looked reproachful. 'If she's all alone, it might be civil.'

'I'd rather not.' Kaye tried to laugh. 'I'm afraid that we don't agree on all counts and she is as likely to want to stay away from me as I am from her. It's been a trying week in many ways, Vincent, and I have a feeling that she would rather be left alone.'

Inwardly she fumed. London was a vast and sprawling city. Why should Orson Latimer haunt her all the way to the West End? And now the one woman she distrusted and disliked was hovering at the side of the hall as if waiting for someone.

'Knowing her, she is likely to have her own

escort,' she said. 'Tony Smythe, the houseman, asked me if I was coming. If he is here, they might well have come together.'

Vincent smiled. 'We might as well get into our seats if you are ready.' He stared. 'There she is.' Kaye pulled on his arm. 'All right, she's gone again, but I think it might have been polite to say hello.' He stiffened. 'Perhaps not. Let's go, Kaye.' He seized her arm and almost thrust her through the crowd as if he had seen the devil.

'Steady! I have high heels,' said Kaye. 'Did you see your bank manager?'

'My bank manager and me are on very good terms. Oh, I see what you mean. What if I did avoid someone?'

'Wouldn't it have been civil to say hello?' said Kaye, smiling.

'Not to this man. To think that he should be here!'

'Who, Vincent?'

'Never you mind. Here, take this programme and tell me if you like the selection.' Vincent glanced back when they were seated and looked up to the upper tiers of the hall and the side seats.

'Sister March is at the back,' he said. 'I imagine that she has an escort as there is a vacant seat beside her.' He continued to stare about him and settled only when the orchestra came on to the stage. Kaye saw him relax, having caught no further glimpse of the man he wanted to avoid.

'I'm glad they are playing some nocturnes,' she whispered. Vincent smiled, pleased that his choice of concert met with such approval. Dinner had been pleasant, with time to chat and to exchange news, and he wondered if Kaye was now ready to think about marriage.

His face hardened. Was it Latimer who he had seen among the people thronging the hall? He dismissed the idea as imagination. The city was crawling with American visitors, French and Swedes, many of them blonde and good-looking and tall. It was a trick of the light and of memory, caused by the fact that Kaye was once more in London, working in the hospital she had left precipitately two years ago. Latimer was in the States. And if he was in the UK again, Kaye had not met him or she would have mentioned it.

The soft music lulled him into peace and, glancing at Kaye, he was glad to see that she sat back with lips slightly parted, absorbing the healing music. They had so much in common; if she would only look forward and forget the past.

A rustle of programmes and a general buzz of conversation formed a prelude to the interval and Vincent forgot that he might have seen Orson Latimer as he pushed through the crowds to fetch the drinks he had ordered and which were set on a long bar with many others, each with a numbered ticket matching the one given at the time the drink was ordered. Kaye followed more slowly, aware that some of the people sitting at the back of the hall had been from the hospital where she was a sister. If Brenda March was one of them, she didn't want to see her.

Vincent beckoned and held out a glass of dry white wine, deliciously cold and exactly what she wanted. Vincent was so good at these things. Doors opened for him and he could get a table in busy restaurants when others were fuming at the door. His air of sleek well-being showed him to be what he was, a wealthy and successful businessman who was used to getting his own way, quietly and with no fuss.

The crowd at the exit thinned as more and more wandered off to explore the rest of the gigantic complex and Vincent basked in the reflected glory of the admiring glances homing in on Kaye. She was just the woman he needed. It was all very well to have her act as hostess when he entertained influential guests, but most of the overseas men took it for granted that they were lovers. It would be better to regularise the situation and enjoy the benefits of marriage.

Kaye stared. Brenda March was looking up into the face of a tall man with fair hair. He had his back towards Kaye and Vincent and she could only guess who it was. Brenda March with Orson, away from the hospital and enjoying a concert together? Kaye put her half-empty glass down on the bar.

'Too dry for you, my dear?' Vincent enquired.

'No, it's fine. Quite delicious,' she said, and picked it up again and made a pretence of enjoying it. Brenda March had been sitting at the back of the hall with an empty seat beside her and Kaye had not noticed who had taken that place. It became more and more apparent that Orson and March were very good friends. She had gone to America to see him, bearing gifts, as he said. She must have known that he was coming back to Beattie's, and now she was making the most of the time she could spend with him. If he was the complete lecher that March had hinted, surely she would avoid such a man, not search him out at every opportunity?

Kaye thought back to the other girls who had followed him around and some of whom he had dated in a casual way when she was not available, and she had to admit that none of those girls had laid any claim to his affections—not for want of trying on their part.

She turned away so that she couldn't see them. What was she trying to do? Was she trying to find excuses for him? He still had the gold pen with the inscription on it from Roma, and the girl in the car earlier in the day, who was on her way back to the States, was very pretty.

The interval bell brought them back to the concert hall and the second half of the programme, but Kaye heard little of the music and her mind formed a knot of confusion and misery. Anyone but March, she thought. Please let it be the American girl if it has to be someone other than me.

Her hands were cold and her throat felt dry, as if she was starting a fever, but she knew that this fever was deep-rooted and would not be resolved by modern drugs. Only the touch of a man with blue eyes and caring hands could heal her, and the scars were deep and went deeper as she thought of him.

'A fine performance,' said Vincent. 'Which piece did you prefer?'

'It's so difficult to say. As you said, it was a fine performance.' How could she make any sensible comment when she had heard so little?

'Harcourt? Kaye Harcourt?' She swung round to see one of the other sisters waving. 'We're having supper before we go back. Want to join us?'

Kaye looked at Vincent and saw that he was

rather relieved to be released early. 'I can take you back if you like,' he began, 'but if you have some-one with you on the way home, I could look in at my office and read the latest telex. I'm expecting news from the Middle East and I would like to check.'

'Of course, Vincent. Even if I was alone, it would be no problem. I can have coffee with them and go when they do. Satisfied?' She gave him a sweet smile and kissed his cheek. 'Good night, Vincent. Thank you for a perfect evening. I have enjoyed every minute.'

He took her hand and pulled her back to him. 'We do get on rather well, darling.'

He kissed her lips and released her with reluct-ance to stand back and watch her go, gracefully weaving a way through the crowd. Then his gaze fixed on the man he had seen earlier and he knew that it was Latimer—but it was only a brief glimpse and he was gone. Vincent swore softly and decided that he must put a little more pressure on Kaye to marry him before that creep showed up again and undid all that time and fresh interests had healed in the past two years.

Kaye found the party of staff from Beattie's and said she would meet them at the entrance. 'Who else is coming?'

'Tony Smythe and Gillian, a girl from the path lab, Brenda March and us. I think that's all. Oh, no, one other man.'

'March?' Kaye tried to smile. 'I must visit the loo. I'll be out there in ten minutes, if that's all right.' She rushed away, filled with panic at the thought of March and the other man coming to join them. Who could it be but Orson Latimer? The fair head was so familiar that she knew she had made no mistake. Wildly, she sought an excuse. For one thing she must avoid bumping into Vincent and letting him know that she was going home alone. And she couldn't face Orson with that woman, not in a social situation.

Kaye dried her hands and opened the door to the wide corridor. Leaning against the wall as if he had all the time in the world to waste, was Orson Latimer. He pulled his hands from his pockets and came towards her. 'Hello,' he said, grinning. 'You took your time in there. I was waiting for you.'

'I can find my own way to meet the others,' she said. 'But you can take a message if you will. I said I'd have supper with them but I really couldn't eat a thing. I had dinner earlier and I think I'd like to get back to the hospital.'

'What others?'

'I thought you were with the other sisters from Beattie's. Tony Smythe is there, too, I believe.'

'No, I'm alone,' he said.

'I'd better get along. They'll wonder where I am,' she said.

'Found your appetite all of a sudden?' Kaye blushed. 'Or can't you bear to be with me for five minutes?'

'It isn't that. I ought to go.'

'Supper with Brenda? Hardly your style, I would have thought. Very attractive in her way but not a woman's woman. I can take that message for you on one condition.' He looked serious. 'I have to talk to you about a case and there hasn't been time lately. I've had other things to do.'

'I shall be on duty tomorrow, in my office. If you

will tell me what notes you will require, I'll see that they are there by ten o'clock.'

He jerked her back as she tried to leave, holding her arm firmly and almost painfully.

'Let me go,' she said.

'Wait here. I mean it, Kaye. I have to talk to you.'

He strode away, confident that she would be there when he returned. The same as ever, she thought. But why should I wait? Anything he has to discuss about the ward can wait and I mustn't let him see that I still love him. She looked round in vain for dear, sweet, safe Vincent. Even Vincent had a certain gleam in his eyes these days, but at least with him she felt safe. But having convinced himself that she was being taken back to the hospital he had left quickly, his mind on the business of the next few days.

A party of Japanese tourists was milling round the foyer, chattering in high, excited voices and pointing out various pieces of modern architecture, and another batch of stolid ladies from a West country women's circle regarded the same things with a mixture of wonder and disapproval. Orson was out of sight and Kaye looked about her for the way out of the entire complex. It was very confusing, as she had learned from others who had been lost on the many badly-signed staircases and levels. She went first in one direction, only to find herself in front of the concert hall again. She changed direction and entered an open area scattered with empty seats and tables loaded with used glasses. She asked two people for help but they smiled and shrugged, understanding nothing of what she said, and she felt like a foreigner in her own country.

At last she saw a sign and followed it. The exit was far from a familiar bus stop or tube station and she began to wish that she had stayed. Orson would be fuming and might even come looking for her, but she had to get away. He had no right to order her to wait and no right to expect her to talk shop when she was off duty.

She bit her lip and hurried into the main thoroughfare where the familiar red buses showed the way to safety. If he had asked her to eat with him, drink with him and to exchange news of their lives since they had parted all that time ago, she might have stayed, with fast-beating heart, to indulge in the sweet agony of his nearness and to see his eyes soften when he looked at her free-flowing hair. But he wasn't interested in her as a woman, unless he could persuade her into bed as just one more easy lay.

The first bus took her some of the way and the underground made the rest of the journey to the Oval easy. Outside again, she looked about her in the neon-studded darkness of the shabby street and to her relief found a taxi. She settled back and sighed, the hidden tension threatening to show as her eyes pricked with distress. What good would she be as a ward sister dealing with suffering and with helpless and sad parents? She must be strong, and if she stayed at the Princess Beatrice in daily contact with Orson, she would have no strength to spare and little compassion for anyone but herself.

The lights in the high wards glowed with the warm reassurance that many felt when they came to the huge mass of building that was the hospital.

Activity inside the driveway, where three ambulances were edging up to the entrance, and the full glare of light in Casualty made her pause to wonder what was being brought in that needed so many vehicles. She walked past the main entrance, as it was a short cut to the side road leading to the new apartment block, and wished that she could lose herself in hard physical work that would leave no time for self-analysis and brooding.

She shivered as she went into the new building. One thin cardigan was not enough in early summer once the sun had gone. Coffee would be nice, she decided, and stopped off in the kitchen where everything necessary was provided. She put on the kettle and found coffee and mugs, looked in the fridge but found no milk or cream and remembered some coffee whitener she had in her room. She left the coffee filtering and went up the stairs to collect the milk powder and a thicker jacket and was on her way down when she heard the telephone.

She smiled. Not for her this time. Vincent would time his call for later, assessing how long it would take her to eat a sandwich and chat in a coffee bar and take the usual route home, but he would want to know that she had returned safely. On another night she might have felt vaguely irritated, cloistered by his over-caring. But tonight she needed to hear his pleasant voice and to know his strength and sheer predictability; he was like a rock to which she could cling when men with stormy eyes threatened her sanity.

The telephone continued to ring and she went back to answer it. Many times others had to do this for her. No one liked taking messages, but it was only fair to take her turn. 'The Princess Beatrice staff hostel,' she said.

'Will you hold the line? I have a person to person call from Boston, USA for Dr Orson Latimer.'

'I'm afraid he isn't available. I think he is still at the Barbican,' she said. 'I'll leave a message that he had a call.'

If it was a person to person call there was no point in asking to speak to the caller, and the last thing that Kaye could bear was to talk to the woman who now filled the life of Dr Orson Latimer. She went to the kitchen and wondered if it was a professional call. Just because she had a fixation about the man didn't mean that he had calls only from beautiful women. Her lips twitched. Even Orson might have to deal with someone who had nothing to offer but advice or medical expertise.

She scribbled a note on a memo pad from her bag and poured out some coffee. She put the note by the telephone, knowing that it was second nature for any member of staff to glance there in case a message had been taken in his or her absence. He was still out or he would have come when the telephone rang. She paused. He might have let it ring, as she had done, hoping it wasn't for someone up on the second floor.

She sipped her coffee. A personal call might be urgent. Bracing herself, she climbed the stairs after checking his room number from the list in the lodge. If he wasn't there, she could put the note under the door. If he was there, she could still push the note under the door! Her courage wasn't high enough to risk a confrontation—not while he was smouldering after she ran out on him. She bent to push the slip of paper under the door, but it was flush with the floor and the paper buckled as she tried to force it through. She stood and smoothed the crumpled scrap and tapped on the door.

Without warning, it was flung open and she was faced with the man who had told her to wait for him. His face was set in an angry frown, and when he saw who was standing there, his eyes blazed with fury.

'Where the hell did you go? I looked all over for you and then went to the coffee bar to see if you'd shown up there.' He flung back his untidy hair, which looked as if he had been rumpling it with frantic fingers.

'I came back by tube,' she said. 'I came up here to tell you that . . .'

'To apologise for wasting my time and energy? For refusing a completely normal request for a talk about something of great importance? Or to tell me that your boyfriend objects to you speaking to me?'

'What's Vincent got to do with it?'

'I saw you taking a very fond farewell. Nice guy. Just the man to look after a fragile creature like you when she comes back after a little fun.'

'You are being very offensive, Orson. Vincent is a very good friend and nothing more.'

'You mean you take your fun elsewhere.' He took her shoulders and shook her roughly. 'I don't get it,' he murmured. 'How can you look as you do when you have no real feelings?'

'You can say that?' Her eyes filled with tears. She was aware of his fingers digging into her soft flesh and his arms drawing her close. She tried to resist but he was far too strong, his brute force over-powering her feeble attempts to escape. His mouth was hard and violent on hers in a kiss that was passion, frustration and fury, no gentle salute of love. She turned her head, straining to escape the insulting embrace.

'I didn't come to apologise,' she gasped. 'There was a telephone call from the States.'

He looked down at her, dazed, as if he surfaced from a dream of violence. Men do crazy things when they look like this, she thought.

'A call from home?'

'I don't know.' She tried to button the front of her dress but found that two buttons were missing, torn off in his groping hands. She pulled the edges together over the mink satin bra and the curve of delicate skin. 'It was a person to person call, so I have no idea who it was. Nor am I interested in which of your women it could have been.'

All her resolutions to be cool and to show no concern about his love life faded and she wanted to scream at him that she wanted him to be hers and hers alone, for ever.

'I see.' The storm had gone and his eyes held a strangely defeated look. He looked at her nearly naked breasts and his mouth tightened. 'Kaye,' he said huskily, but she fled back to her room, slamming the door and locking it before he could catch up with her. She heard him tapping with the persistence of one who knows she must give in and she trembled and sat on the bed, staring at the locked door. The tapping stopped abruptly and she heard the telephone ringing again. She unlocked the door and went out on to the landing. He was down in the hall, lifting the receiver, and she bent shamelessly down to listen.

'Hello,' he said. 'Sure I'll take the call.' Kaye crept down lower on the stairs behind a bend where she was hidden from the hall. 'Roma? Hello, honey.' He listened. 'Yes, I know it's been a long time. Sure! Now listen. You can't come now. The time isn't right. I have to organise something and you can't come here. It just wouldn't do, honey. I'll call you in a day or so, say Friday, ten p.m. British time? I promise that I'll have news for you then and I can't wait to get you here with everything settled.' He sighed. 'I know, I know. It can't be long now. Sleep tight, honey.'

Kaye crept back to her room and locked the door again, but although she lay awake for hours, Orson made no further effort to get into her room. If he could have done so, he would have raped me, she thought, her eyelids stiff with tears. And yet he switched away from me to calm down another woman who seems to be chasing him and for whom he has either lost interest and is trying to shake off—or perhaps she is someone he loves and he is secretly involved with her in a liaison that will soon be made public.

CHAPTER FIVE

'DID you see Simon?' Dr Ben Hanley smiled and the new Sister on the children's ward knew that he was very excited. 'You know, the first child we had in here several years ago. He came in for checks and a final blood test and also to appear on a medical science documentary this afternoon. We shall have TV cameras all over the place.' He tried to look serious. 'Perfect nuisance, of course, but in a way we are making history.'

'You mean he is one of your pituitary hormone deficiency children?' Kaye asked.

'Yes, he came in measuring at least four inches shorter than his sister, who is two years younger. The atmosphere at school was getting him down.' He looked round the peaceful ward with affection. 'Children can be so cruel at times, but it made him very determined to do everything we told him and after his course of hormones he grew steadily and is now as tall as Rachel, his sister.'

Dr Hanley put down the folder of notes. 'I really haven't time to continue the round, Sister. Dr Latimer will be coming down and he can do what is necessary.'

'Dr Latimer?'

'Yes, he's back now, working with the team and with the Maple Syrup Syndrome set. Be nice to him—I think he might be jet-lagged after a late flight last night from Boston.'

99

'I see,' was all Kaye could say. Ben Hanley gave her a sharp look. 'Isn't it odd to be on two such teams?'

'Not usual, but not unknown,' he said. 'Orson asked to widen his experience and as we are one of the few centres examining the syndrome, he wants to be in the picture to take the information back to the States when he leaves for good in a couple of months time.' He looked reflective. 'We are due to admit three children and there is pressure to take one from the States again. That gets tricky as many people think we should concentrate on our own nationals first. A bit selfish, especially as we have a free interchange of discovered knowledge and the Yanks give us good stuff in their turn.'

'Yes, I do see that,' said Kaye Harcourt. 'Do you think Dr Latimer will give the nurses a lecture on it? Tony Smythe is very good but he doesn't make it plain and I haven't the full back-up of test results to make what I say very convincing. So many of the children were here before I came back and I haven't time to read up all the series, but anyone coming in on the medical side would need to do so.'

His face cleared. 'I began to think you would not co-operate with Orson. I'm glad that you've made it up.'

'I co-operate with him on everything to do with the ward, Dr Hanley, but it doesn't mean we see each other outside working hours.' She hesitated. 'In any case, he hasn't been on the ward for days. I wondered if he had gone for good.'

'No, he had a rather hysterical cable and rushed for the first plane available.' Ben shrugged. 'Don't ask me what it was all about, but he was always a bit on the impulsive side, wasn't he?'

Instinctively, Kaye's hand went to her shoulder where the remnants of Orson's bruising grasp had left a mark. 'You could say that,' she said.

'I shall want you to appear in the TV film of course, Sister,' Ben Hanley laughed. 'Orders from Jill. She said I must include you to show what glamorous girls we have on the staff here. You are to be in the ward when the cameras are turning.'

'I can't. I wasn't involved with the first cases.'

'You are now, and the sister who was here is nursing in Timbuctoo or somewhere like it and we can't ask her to fly over for half an hour.' He eyed Kaye with affection. 'Besides, you are so good with the children. They are quiet and good when you are here. We shall be starting after lunch. Is that convenient? Or have the other firms anything horrific happening?'

'No tonsils today, and several children for discharge. If the out-patients with PHS come up at one, they can play in the day room and it will look as if they are already here as patients.' She smiled. 'I'll make sure that everything looks right. By the way, what happened to Michelle? I know she went out and I was worried about her.'

'I saw the parents and her aunt, who is a very humane and homely woman. They agreed to let Michelle go to her for a while and in time, I think, they may let her adopt the child—and her sister, who is in Care.'

Dr Hanley gazed at a mark on the wall left by a too-enthusiastic artist of five years of age. 'It's strange how some people can love and care for their children very well indeed, but dislike one—or in this instance, the two girls. The boys are well and happy, if a bit rough like the father, but the little girls could be in danger if they were sent back again. If they have a happy home with the aunt, they might well grow to like their father when they are older. It never ceases to surprise me what happens within families.'

He laughed. 'We all have hidden depths, I suppose. Some men are womanisers and some beat their wives, and it isn't always the ones you would suspect who do so. A big man who seems powerful can be the gentlest creature.'

'A tame bull?' she said. 'But can you be sure?'

He pushed the folder into her hands, apologising for rushing away, and she was left to brace herself for the visit of the American doctor. Nelson Charumbera came into the ward.

'Hello, are you fit again? I have a few notes for you to sign and some drugs to write up,' Kaye greeted him.

'I knew it.' He groaned but took a seat at the desk. 'Ask now. If I appear as a film star, you can hope for nothing,' he said.

'You look better. Can you do the round before the TV people come?' He grinned and pulled the prescription pad towards him. 'I'll send in some coffee,' Kaye added, willing him to finish the round and to make any help from Dr Latimer superfluous. 'You will have time to have lunch and to put on your most photogenic tie.'

'Why the hurry, Sister?'

'We ought to be clear before the cameras are here. If anything is left, we might miss something important,' she said. He sighed and looked at the notes.

'Bless you,' she said, and went out to ask the junior to tidy the day room and to set up some impressive building bricks.

The hands of the ward clock crept on and Kaye began to relax. If Dr Latimer came now, he would find the notes written, the drugs ordered and treatments done, the ward tidy and nothing needed. As usual, Nelson had done his work quickly and efficiently and made several solemn faces smile.

Sandwiches came up from the general kitchen for the technicians who were arranging lights to the delight of three small boys who were anxious to help, and Kaye decided that her lunch would have to be forgotten. She made coffee and sampled the sandwiches, keeping an eye on the progress being made, and by one o'clock the ward had an air of busy tranquillity. Lunch for the children was over and cleared and some special treats had been lined up for later.

One boy sat bolt upright on his bed and seemed slightly scared of the men trailing wires and talking in loud voices. He had been admitted the day before and was waiting for an operation on his ears. Poor little Dumbo; that was the usual name given him and Sister Harcourt was filled with compassion for the boy whose ears stuck out almost at right angles. He must have suffered agonies, she thought, now that he was old enough to know what people said about his appearance.

She stood by him and gave him a bright book to read, but as she moved away he began to cry. Out of the corner of her eye she saw Dr Hanley come into the ward with the producer, a young trendy who looked completely out of place in this setting and might expect everyone to act on cue, including small boys with sticky-out ears who wanted their mum!

In the background Kaye saw Nelson Charumbera appear with a video camera slung on his shoulder, following the movements of the film crew who had started their work. Obviously the hospital team intended making a record of their work for their own use.

She also saw Orson Latimer hovering in the background, and Dr Hanley turning to bring him into the circle of discussion, now being filmed. Michael opened his mouth and made it a neat, large empty square, but before he uttered the loud cry that Sister Harcourt expected, she scooped him out of bed and cradled him in her arms. The cry never surfaced and he clung to her, snuggling close and looking into her face.

'Hush,' she said. 'It's all right. If you keep very quiet, you might be on telly.' He opened his eyes wide and watched the men in white coats and the camera crew from the safety of her softness, and as the cameras scanned the ward for good shots, they homed in on a sweet, dignified madonna, holding a rather odd looking child. Orson Latimer stared and had to drag his attention back to the discussion.

'I'm going to put you down now, Michael. Watch the camera and smile,' Kaye said, aware that the camera had been on her for far longer than she liked. She turned her back slightly and the lens went on to other beds and the group of children by the table, all of whom were pituitary hormone cases. She felt herself blushing.

The camera session ended, and the producer was delighted. He had the right mix of drama and serious professional data in the rather poignant children who would be sentimentalised in the voice-over, to be added to the finished documentary, and a bonus of a rather beautiful girl holding a child in her arms. Terrific!

'Now we can get back to work,' said Sister Harcourt firmly, in an effort to tear the nursing staff away from dreams of stardom.

'Thank you for keeping everything calm, Sister.' Dr Hanley smiled. 'Publicity can do nothing but good,' he said. 'We need people to know of our work and to give freely when we hold the next appeal for funds.'

Kaye tried to look unconcerned, but she recalled the look that Orson Latimer had in his eyes when he watched her across the ward and she wanted to get away from him as soon as possible. He stood behind Dr Hanley, looming over him and saying nothing, but his presence was enough without words. Kaye could feel the current of feeling between them and wondered if he saw the hidden emotions that she tried to control. He wanted her still, after all this time. That had been clear when he kissed her fiercely outside his room, and when he watched her in the ward.

I could smile at him now and lose my soul, she thought. So easy to do. Just accept that he wants my body and my nursing expertise and there is no need for deeper feelings; just animal passion and satisfaction in work. She bent to pick up a doll that a child had treated as a football and when she looked up he was examining some notes and seemed fully absorbed.

Dr Charumbera went up to him. 'Here is the video camera back, Dr Latimer.' So the video equipment was Orson's!

'I wondered what you were doing with that,' Dr Hanley said curiously.

'I asked if I could have a copy of the film for my own purposes,' Orson explained, 'but that would have meant a wait. This way we can view it immediately. If you'll excuse me, sir, I'll just go and fix it up—then we can all see it.'

'Fine. And after that we must talk about your future plans with Roma,' Dr Hanley said.

'I'm really very grateful. I know she will be too.' Orson Latimer smiled and looked very young and delighted. 'Your approval means we can go ahead and she can make plans.'

'We have to keep our men happy,' said Dr Hanley.

Kaye Harcourt busied herself with the mangled bedclothes of a tiny girl who liked to lie face down at the wrong end of her bed. If I had smiled and invited him to come closer, that would have been another humiliation, she thought. Would he really be so insensitive and cruel as to bring a girl over from the States and marry her within news-carrying distance of the hospital and all its gossip?

At least he wasn't involved with March, but the knowledge gave Kaye no real satisfaction. She had tried to think that an American girl would hurt less, but it wasn't so. Her heart and mind were filled with sadness, deep lost love and bitter jealousy.

'If you don't need me, I think I'll go off duty. I have to be back this evening and I have some letters to write.'

'I'm sorry if you are late, Sister, but we couldn't have done without you. I'll come across with you, if I may, and have a quick look at some of the tape. Orson should have it fixed by now. I'm sure that you are as interested as we are, as you were on film for a very long time.' Dr Hanley laughed. 'I think the cameraman forgot that he was filming children and pleased himself!'

'They can cut out me when they edit,' Kaye said. There was no escape. She had hoped to slip into the hostel and up to her room without being seen. But now, with Ben Hanley on her tail, she would have to go to the room where Orson lived and make polite conversation.

'It's really quite warm,' she said as they walked over to the block. 'I'm dying for some country air. One of the parents invited us to his house-warming. I might go down early and walk for a while. Sister Kingston wants to go to the farm and it does sound rather nice.'

'You mean the Roccos? He's in pharmaceuticals, you know. I met him at a congress last year. You'll like his family.' He thought for a while. 'Jill did say something about an invitation. It's going to be a big affair. Maybe we'll see you there if my diary allows it.'

'I had no idea that he had other links with medicine. When he came here he was just another anxious parent—more anxious, in fact, as he has a rather volatile temperament.'

'I can imagine. He has great enthusiasms that

flare up and then are forgotten. The farm is one that seems permanent. He wants to be the perfect English gentleman farmer, and send his children to school here, but he needs excitement and I can't see it lasting. He's more the type to roam vast ranches in South America, not farm the gentle Surrey hills.'

'Someone said he might raise horses. That fits the open-air image, doesn't it?'

'Much more likely than totting up milk yields. Here we are. I must say they've done the staff well this time. When I was climbing drain-pipes into nurses' rooms, the accommodation was very poor.'

'You climbed drain-pipes?' She laughed. 'Is that how you courted Jill?'

'Well, the rules were much stuffier then. Back at ten or some ungodly hour, and no male visitors in rooms after that time. It was an invitation to illicit sex—everyone knew that it was safe to stay quietly in a girl's room until after the home sister made her locking-up round at eleven. After that, it was easy to shin down on to the lodge roof and away to the medical school at any time after midnight.'

'It's quite different now. People come and go and medical staff live in the same buildings as nursing staff. Nobody notices if staff are in or out. But of course, we impress on nurses in training that they must be alert and rested when they go on duty or they pick up infections and lack concentration. That can be bad if they aren't sensible, but I think that, having liberty, they adjust and probably don't use it unwisely. After a busy day on a ward, the greatest luxury is a bath and bed . . . alone.'

'I'm sure you're right, and it does allow people like you to entertain friends and colleagues in a perfectly normal way, without anyone reading more into a relationship than exists,' Dr Hanley agreed.

'It doesn't work all the time. There are people who would make scandal out of a cup of tea in the garden.'

He gave her a shrewd look. 'You said that with feeling. I do know. I hear more than I ought sometimes and I have learned over the years who can be trusted with a confidence and who stirs up trouble.' They went up the stairs. 'Which room is Latimer's?'

'He's on the next floor.' Kaye saw him smile. 'I had to take a telephone message for him and I checked the list by the phone. That at least hasn't changed, I suspect. Everyone tries to ignore the telephone in case they have to run up two flights of stairs with a message for someone they don't even know—and then can't find the room.'

'That is the same as in my time, but I was near the phone and could chat up other men's girlfriends and sometimes date them if they were sufficiently annoyed with their men.'

'You must have been a very devious student and *very* enterprising,' Kaye laughed. 'That is the room,' she said, pointing to an open door.

The television set was in full view and the picture was static, as if Orson Latimer had frozen one particular frame. He sat on the bed staring at it and Kaye wanted to pull Ben Hanley away and retreat, to save her own embarrassment. Orson seemed not to hear them until Ben Hanley spoke.

'That really is quite a picture,' he said. Orson Latimer bent forward and the film began again at speed, a blur of movement and colour until it came to the end of the reel. 'Oh, why do that? I wanted a closer look. Sişter Harcourt should audition for films. You have a very lovely profile, my dear.' He seemed to feel the tension in the room. 'Can we run through the first bit where you diścuss the syndrome with the pathologist?'

Dr Hanley turned to Kaye. 'I should go and write those letters. No doubt Orson will give us all a showing soon and you needn't waste your off duty.'

She fled and sat in her room, watching but not seeing the leaves of the cherry trees in the park, on the other side of the garden wall. He had her picture to stare at as often as he pleased, to want and yet not to love, as a man gazes at an erotic picture or a stolen work of art—a hidden fantasy. He would gaze at her holding the child in her arms and think that she was false, a mask hiding a fickle and promiscuous heart.

She tried to write to her cousin but the page remained empty after ten minutes. He had been with March at the concert, even if she wasn't with him after the evening ended, and March would lose no chance of digging at her reputation once more. Kaye looked through several copies of the *Nursing Mirror*, hoping to see a job advertised that would compare favourably with her present one, but she wanted to stay at the hospital she loved, not be driven out into the wilderness by one bitter, lying tongue and one man who threatened her.

She went to the cafeteria for tea and met Ercil Kingston. 'You are coming to the farm, aren't you?'

'Yes, I couldn't resist the idea of a real country walk and if we can think up a way of getting there and back it should be good.'

'Mrs Hanley rang the ward and asked if we were going. She is driving down as she is a friend of the family as well as being connected through the hospital. She offered to pick us up and bring us back.'

'She's a pet,' said Kaye warmly.

'She said she'd be glad of the company if her husband can't make it.'

'I'd certainly like the lift back, but I wanted to go early, as it will be my day off, and walk on the Downs.'

'You could take the train to Guildford and we could pick you up—we have to pass through there on the way. If you say a time—or I suppose we'd better leave it to her to do that, as it's her car and time we're using—then you can be there, waiting to thumb a lift,' Ercil suggested.

'Fine. I'll go back to the home and phone her now. I'll let you know what she says and then you can make your arrangements. It takes all the hassle out of the outing if we can be sure of getting back again.'

'We wouldn't be stranded. Mr Rocco tried to persuade me to spend the weekend there, and as many of Beattie's staff who wanted a break in the country. He really does go over the top, that man. I'd hate to be on the receiving end of his gratitude if his son had to be in for months.'

Kaye went back to her room to find Jill's telephone number, which was ex-directory for the sake of Ben's privacy when off duty. She went down to the deserted hall and rang the number, and was soon chatting to her friend.

'Of course it's no bother. I only wish I could come earlier and walk with you. Where do you think you'll go?' Jill asked.

'I might take the train to Box Hill and have lunch in the motel there, or the old coaching house in the town. From there I can bus to Guildford and look round until you pick me up at six. If the weather holds it should be lovely. It might even be an early hay-making after this dry spell. I shall drink in the sight of young beech woods and the scent of summer.'

'Ben might come too, but you know how it is. If I didn't make my own arrangements I would have to take up crochet or make endless pots of jam, and I don't even like jam!'

'One of the few disadvantages of marrying a famous paediatrician,' Kaye sympathised,'

'You wait until it happens to you. Part of the time it is heaven and then there are long periods when work comes first. Being in the same trade, I know that it is inevitable. I sometimes think I shall do some part-time work in a clinic.'

'It isn't likely to happen to me. I am concentrating on the ward at present.'

'And Vincent? He's still around?'

'Oh yes, he is, but if I married him I would never have to put sick children before a social life. It's more likely that I would spend my time trying to make myself understood entertaining far-Eastern business men and brushing up my French and Italian.'

'Sounds good,' said Jill wistfully.

'Only with the right man,' said Kaye, 'and I'm not sure that I could make him happy.'

'I did have other ideas for you, Kaye, but you don't seem to fall in with them.'

'It's no good, Jill. I aim to work hard and to take a sister tutor's exam next year if possible. That way I could move around, see the world and be free.'

Kaye heard a movement behind her and glanced up. Orson Latimer stood by the table, reading a letter he held in his hand. The envelope lay on the table and as Kaye said goodbye to Jill he stepped forward, the letter still in his hand. He smiled briefly and dialled a number. Kaye passed the table and the breeze from the outer door, suddenly rushing in as a nurse ran by, sent the envelope to the floor. Instinctively she picked it up and noted that it had come by airmail from the States. On the back was the name and address of the sender. Roma Sterling.

Kaye pictured the kind of woman she was. If it was the girl in the car, she was beautiful and young; but surely she was very demanding, ringing up so often, sending hysterical cables and writing as soon as she returned, expecting him to ring as soon as her letter arrived.

It's none of my business, she told herself firmly. He has girlfriends all over the place, so why not from his home town? It was more likely to be a serious affair leading to marriage if it happened under the eyes of his local family friends.

At least he was occupied for a while, the ward work was done and Dr Charumbera was back on duty to cope with the daily routine and notes. He can go back to doing a night round and not appearing during the day, she thought resentfully. She sighed. I'm unhappy if I don't see him, and when I do I freeze up and feel terrible, afraid of showing even a shred of normal friendship in case he thinks I'm encouraging him. And we used to work so well together.

The children were noisier than usual when she went back on duty, each one telling their visitors that they had been on television, even if they had not appeared on the film. The finished documentary wouldn't be shown for a long time and mothers and fathers were suitably impressed. Gradually the ward became quiet, the lights were dimmed and the small humps in the beds and cots lay still or twitched in dreams. Kaye checked two babies who were due for heart operations the next day and would go to Intensive Care for a while before returning to the ward. They were asleep but breathing lightly, one with her tiny nose pinched in an effort to take in more oxygen and the other slightly blue-lipped.

A few years ago such operations would have had their own drama, but now they were almost routine and had a high success rate, leading to a healthy, full life and no bad complications. Kaye tucked the sheet more firmly under one small chin and stood admiring a girl with long golden curls and bright cheeks who lay in a plaster cast after a car accident. She was recovering well enough to be out of the cast for hours at a time, but slept in it at night.

If Orson had children, they would be blonde, clear-eyed and beautiful, very American and self-assured. Kaye lifted the bedclothes gently to make sure that the child was lying evenly in the cast and stepped back. It was useless getting maudlin about other people's children and imagining the never-to-be.

'She's kinda cute,' said Orson quietly. 'Be playing basketball again in a few weeks.'

'Netball,' Kaye corrected, and blushed. It had been one of their teasing jokes that American children played basketball, watched ice-hockey and the ball game and English children played hockey and football and rugby and netball.

'Not this one. Look at her, she's a perfect cheer leader, a born majorette.'

'If you like that kind of child. Much too exhibitionist for me.' She tried to walk away but he stood in front of her and was far too big to push away or to walk over.

'Excuse me, I have a report to write and I promised to lecture the nurses if they finish in time.'

'I can do that. Ben Hanley asked me to tell them about Maple Syrup Syndrome.' He didn't move. 'Why did you run out on me, Kaye? I told you to wait.'

'Yes, you told me,' she said. 'Well, I am here, ready to talk shop on duty in the right surroundings.'

'You've grown hard,' he said.

'If you say so,' she replied, and he let her go, following her back to the office. 'What was it you wanted to discuss that has relevance to these children, Dr Latimer?'

Two nurses were ready for report and he glanced at them, wishing them out of the office but not able to dismiss them. 'It stems from the Maple Syrup Syndrome,' he said.

The junior nurse looked up with sparkling eyes. 'Oh, I *am* glad I'm on duty if you are giving us a lecture.'

Kaye smiled and found that she exchanged an amused glance with Orson, as they used to do. One thing he didn't do; even if he had many conquests among the staff, he was no cradle-snatcher.

'And you'd better listen,' he said in mock severity. The other nurses came in and Kaye sat back at a small table with the report book, but she found it impossible to concentrate for long as she watched his mobile lips and listened to the firm, warm voice with the trace of accent she had once found endearing.

'I'll put it very simply.' He looked round at the intent faces. 'In some children, certain amino acids that are essential to life are not absorbed and are excreted in the urine, giving the urine a typical smell similar to maple syrup. Don't confuse it with diabetes, when patients have ketosis and breath smelling of new-mown hay. You sure need a sense of smell to be a nurse.'

A ripple of amusement went round the room. Two points they will never forget as they were told in a conversational way, thought Kaye, making a valiant effort to write.

'Now write this down and learn it. The names of the amino acids are leucine, isoleucine and valine. When this syndrome occurs the babies get the twitches and have feeding difficulties. They breathe badly and there is often damage to the central nervous system. Get the picture?' They nodded.

'A diet low in the three amino acids is given and is

effective if started early, but they need regular checks and that means coming back to the clinic for screening twice a year or more. Some children come from long distances, even from the States as this place and, primarily, Great Ormond Street, are the centres for the scientific work involved. The simple treatment is effective and life saving.' He glanced across at Kaye who was bent over her book.

'I have a friend who is involved with this as a parent. I know what it means to know there are places like this.'

The nurses looked at him wide-eyed and impressed. He has a magic, thought Kaye, and it's making them all want to work with him, to be close to him, and much more.

She took her report book to the desk area along the corridor as she knew she could never finish it coherently if she stayed listening to his voice. The night staff came by as she finished and closed the book. She walked back with the staff nurse and saw a white coat through the frosted glass panels of her office. Orson came towards her, frowning as if he thought she might be alone. The night nurse sat in her usual seat waiting for report and Kaye saw Dr Latimer's face harden.

If he thinks I'm avoiding him, he's right, thought Kaye with a tinge of triumph. I have my work to do and well he knows it.

'Right, Nurse,' she said. 'I'll get report over and take you to see the latest admissions. Dr Charumbera is back and has done all the notes and the drug list has been revised. I made out a new one as there were so many children discharged who no longer had medicine here that it was becoming confusing.'

Orson Latimer shifted from one foot to the other and looked at his watch. 'Sister Harcourt, could I have a word with you?'

'Certainly,' she said briskly and looked up, smiling. 'Stay there, Nurse. I haven't finished with you.'

He looked annoyed. 'I need to talk to you.'

'Right. Here I am. The notes about your babes are over there and the fresh reports are in that folder.'

He looked at his watch again. 'Could you spare ten minutes?' he grated.

'I shall be off duty in fifteen minutes and I can remain here in the office after that time, if that will do.'

The bleeper in his pocket shrilled softly and he swore. 'I have to go. I can't wait now.'

'If it's a long distance call, I should hurry,' she said sweetly. Only one woman could make him like a cat on hot bricks awaiting her call. Only one woman would telephone all the way from the States so often and send cables to keep him in line. They stared at each other for a full minute. 'Go on,' she said. 'I think you are wanted.'

'Just as well,' he said softly as he passed her chair. 'I can see that I am not wanted here.'

She finished report and afterwards could not recall going round the ward with the night nurse, but outwardly everything must have been normal or she would have been given some peculiar looks. 'I'm sorry we missed hearing Dr Latimer,' said the night staff nurse. 'He is the best looking man we've seen in Beattie's for ages.' She eyed Sister Harcourt with speculation. 'He isn't married, is he?'

'Why not ask him?' Sister smiled without humour. 'I honestly couldn't tell you anything about his love life, Nurse, but you must remember that he comes from the States and may have a wife or fiancée over there.'

'Sister March said . . .' The girl blushed.

'Ask her. She was with him at the concert, I believe. I'm sure that after an hour of Chopin he would have softened up and confided in her.'

The nurse laughed. 'Sister March does like to know everything.' She looked puzzled. 'But she doesn't know about him, or why should she ask us who sees him on the ward?'

'Perhaps he will surprise us all.' Kaye put down the chart from the last bed and looked down at Michael, glad that he was sleeping peacefully with no idea of what would happen tomorrow. The operation would not give him much discomfort, as it only entailed the surgeon cutting and removing a slice of the resilient cartilage from each flap and sewing it closer to his head. It was clean surgery with no risk of infection or pain and the stitches would be out in a few days.

'He'll look quite pretty,' she said. 'Poor little fellow, he should have been done ages ago.'

Ercil would be off duty and they could discuss the trip down to the farm in Surrey before Kaye started her day off and Ercil was back on duty. It would be so good to get away and to forget Orson Latimer and everything that darkened her enjoyment of the ward. Kaye thought of the video film and wanted to take it from his room and destroy it. She felt vulnerable, knowing that he could see her and linger over each frame, assessing her face and body like a voyeur who kept pictures of women for his private delight. She had to see that she was over-reacting. At least they weren't nude pictures but demurely uniformed shots of a professional nursing sister. There was nothing wrong in that.

But she had seen the frozen frame with the child caressing the outline of her breast and the expression that spoke of tenderness in her own eyes, and she knew that Orson Latimer could look into her heart, see the woman under the crisp uniform and doubt that she had grown hard with no more love to give.

'Let's walk across the park and have supper in the Falcon,' said Ercil. 'I couldn't face shop talk in the dining-room tonight.'

'Good idea,' said Kaye with a sensation of release. 'I haven't been there since I left two years ago.'

'It's changed a lot,' said Ercil. 'When I saw it first, I recall that it had two bars and a lot of staring locals who thought that any woman alone in a bar was a tart.' She laughed. 'Now they don't turn a hair if a woman is alone, or if she is black, white or khaki—and the punks sit outside in fine weather, adding a bit of atmosphere!' She laughed. 'Don't be put off. The Peregrine bar is very good and fairly plush, and the new carvery is useful when my man comes to see me and we want to eat and talk at leisure—and of course, it has become the local club of most of Beattie's staff.'

The park retained its Victorian dignity, slightly decayed but full of colour, with banks of rhododendrons moving softly in the breeze and making a backdrop to the elaborate stonework bordering the paths. A man walked ahead of the two girls, almost lost in the dim light that blurred the colour and the memories of the place.

Kaye was glad that the dusk hid most of the places she associated with Orson, and knew that she must come to terms with the fact that over there, she had once studied, sitting in the alcove of pale stone with its arched canopy and gargoyle heads. Orson had found her very often and interrupted her work, bringing her silly gifts of magnolia petals wrapped in big leaves, caterpillars and centipedes to scare her into his arms and his light tantalising kisses, that promised so much and held back even more as she looked into his eyes. It was as if he held a precious porcelain figure that he wanted very badly but knew he could not possess until it was really his by right.

For a man like Orson, who took what he wanted from life and usually didn't have to ask twice, this had been a revelation and nothing had convinced Kaye more of his love for her than this attitude. Until, that was, rumours of his amours filtered through to her and rumours of her weekends with Vincent had made him madly jealous and cruel, accepting no excuse and looking on her with wounded pride and disillusionment. How much influence March had on him even now was hard to guess, but Kaye had seen him with the pretty American, heard his tender voice on the telephone when he spoke to her or another woman and read the inscription on the pen that Roma had given him.

She and Ercil went into the lounge bar and found seats by the window. The fresh scent of leaves and the last of the wallflowers came up through the open window, but Ercil shivered. 'Do you mind? I can't get used to the British fetish for fresh air.'

'I'll do it, but you'll be sorry when the evening fug gets going. I shall have enough fresh air when I go walking tomorrow. I'm looking forward to my first free day, and the evening sounds jolly interesting.'

They ordered baked potatoes stuffed with ham and mushrooms and chive butter and drank dry cider. It was a new angle to London and one that appealed to Kaye after her sadness of the past few days, and it was with reluctance that she suggested they go back to the hospital, knowing that Ercil was on early duty and had a very busy morning ahead.

'I want to book a table for next week when we come for lunch. It gets very crowded and we don't like to waste time queuing,' said Ercil. 'Time is precious now that my boyfriend is busy and we like to make the most of it. I'll slip into the carvery and see the manager and you can wait in the entrance when you are ready.'

Ercil walked away, her tall, graceful figure proud and erect and her rather long neck supporting the fine-boned head and lovely features. Many people glanced at her as she passed. Kaye smoothed down her full skirt and picked up her handbag, which matched the dark brown suede of her jacket. The mixture of flame and ochre in the soft woollen

material in her skirt and lambswool sweater gave
her an air of elegant understatement over which her
pale skin and dark hair and eyes bloomed with a
radiance as soft as the glow on a lustre vase.

She followed Ercil as far as the door but went on
to the entrance, sniffing the freshness of the night.
She pulled her jacket round her. Ercil would
grumble all the way back. She was a hot-house
flower who hated the cold, and the night was
turning chilly.

Kaye glanced at her watch and wondered what
was keeping her friend so long. She looked back
and saw her with a man who was the complete foil
to her darkness. Kaye felt her spirits plummet and
her heart beat with a deep and painful metre. She
had seen the man walking through the park and
wondered if it was Orson, but that man had turned
under a lamp and she had seen his face and known
that it was one of the other registrars on a firm that
she knew only vaguely. Somehow, seeing him had
made her believe that if that wasn't Orson Latimer,
she was safe from him during the evening. How
wrong can I be? she thought as he came towards
her.

He smiled politely and Ercil said, 'Dr Latimer is
going to save me from freezing and take us back by
car.'

'How kind,' said Kaye, looking at him with cool
indifference.

'Not if you feel safer in the park, alone with all
the late night drunks,' he said.

'No, I think you might be quite safe,' she said.
'Unless you have forgotten how to drive on the left
side of the road?'

'I have forgotten nothing about this country or the people in it,' he said.

'Not even the fairytales?' she murmured to herself, but his face gave no indication that he had heard.

Orson Latimer unlocked the car and Ercil slipped into the back seat. Kaye made as if to follow but he held the front passenger door open in a way that made it impossible for her to do anything but sit by his side. She sat down and he bent to pick up the trailing edge of her skirt before he closed the door. A lump in her throat threatened to choke her. It had always been so. It was an instinctive caring gesture, but this time his hand lingered as it touched her thigh and she knew a sensation of languorous bliss spread over her whole body.

Swiftly, he went round to the driver's seat and slammed the door after him. It took less then ten minutes to reach the main gates of the hospital and Ercil protested that they could walk through to the hostel if he had things to do in the main block, but he insisted on driving them to the front door.

'Could you give Dr Hanley a message tomorrow?' he asked. 'I shall be away for the day and doubt if I shall see him when he comes in.'

'I can leave a note,' said Kaye. 'I have a day off tomorrow and aim to leave early.'

'I see.' His profile was set. 'Where is he taking you this time?'

'Who?'

'Vincent.' The way he said it was almost an insult, as if the name was fit only for derision.

'I'm not seeing Vincent,' she said. 'Is it so difficult to believe that I can entertain myself on occasion? Vincent and I are very good friends.'

'I noticed,' he said.

'Everyone has friends,' she said, trying to keep her cool, 'but some are very dear and lasting and have no hang-ups.' She glanced at him. 'Some friends have trust and only believe about half of what they are told, if it is bad.'

'And some have no sense because they care.' It was a whisper that she could only strive to catch but of which she wasn't sure.

'We're here,' said Ercil, tired of sitting in the car now that it had been at a halt for at least two minutes. She struggled with the door. 'Have you got kiddie locks on this car? I can't get out.'

Orson went to her aid and Kaye dropped her handbag on the floor as she tried to open her door. She groped for it and found that several items had fallen on the floor, and she pushed them back into the side pocket. She groped again to make sure she had everything and snapped the bag shut. Orson opened her door and put out a hand to help her out. She felt again the firm warm grasp and longed for the insecure haven of his arms, the taurean strength and the force of his love, but instead she thanked him for the lift and escaped to her room, knowing that his eyes were bleak with angry suspicion, as they had been when they parted so long ago. How could he be like that when he had so many other women in his life? Was there still one rule for the chauvinistic male and one for the docile little woman in the background?

Kaye turned her handbag up and tipped out the contents. After being spilled, it needed sorting and she put back the coin purse, the wallet and note-book but saw that the pen was still missing. She had also picked up something that didn't belong to her. It was an envelope addressed to Orson Latimer and on the back was a name and address, exactly the same as the one she had seen a few days ago. It had a more recent date than the last she had picked up and, to her intense relief, there was no letter in the envelope. If there had been, it would have been more than human frailty could stand. She would have had to read it.

She put it in another envelope and addressed it to Orson Latimer, then slipped down to put it in his pigeon-hole in the lodge. Anyone could have found the old envelope and picked it up, and she wanted no contact, no comment on the ownership of the notepaper.

'Roma,' she kept saying to herself. 'Why Roma?' Was she engaged to him?

Kaye snatched up the telephone as it rang. The American voice was soft and rather pleasant and asked for Dr Latimer. She turned and he was there. Dumbly she handed him the phone and, as he took it, he grinned and kissed her cheek. Kaye stepped back, her shock showing in her eyes. What had happened to him that he could know that she had listened to the voice of the woman he loved and yet could still steal a kiss before speaking to Roma as if neither woman was of paramount importance? It was only later that she recalled that Roma was telephoning from this country and not from the States.

So now she is here, Kaye thought. No wonder he is away tomorrow.

CHAPTER SIX

KAYE HARCOURT turned her face to the sun and breathed in the sharp sweet smell of young leaves. Looking up through the filigree of beech branches she could see the blue sky patched with thin white cloud. She was slightly out of breath and looked down at the hill she had climbed and the wide view of the Surrey she had once known so well. The lump of stone half-buried in the soil made a welcome seat and she was glad to sit for a while on something that wouldn't be damp and uncomfortable, as the soft grass and earth would be.

She was free at last and she began to enjoy the day. The hospital was far away and from here she could think about the people who troubled her and invaded her life. She looked at her watch. Although she had started early and was lucky with buses, it was nearly lunch-time, and the note that Ercil left for her had said one-thirty at the motel carvery. Kaye could see the hotel far below and stood up, brushing away dry leaves from her heather tweed skirt and the suede jacket and boots. She smiled. Ercil was always in a rush. She'd left just a cryptic note saying the time and place and made no attempt to check if Kaye could be there. But it was nice that she had managed to get the extra time off to join her at Box Hill.

Kaye began to walk down slowly. If she was off duty, why couldn't Ercil have come with her this morning and enjoyed the walk? It couldn't be that she might put out the arrangement made with Jill Hanley, for the lunch date would interfere with that in any case. I hope she rang Jill to say she wouldn't need that lift until she picks us both up in Guildford, Kaye thought. She hurried. If Ercil was there waiting, she could phone from the motel to make sure that Jill wasn't inconvenienced.

The lower slopes were smooth and it seemed a pity to leave. What did lunch matter on a fine day? Ercil would want to sit in a closed room, oblivious to the tobacco smoke and stuffy atmosphere, wanting only to be warm. That's why she didn't come with me, thought Kaye. She couldn't face the cool breeze on the hill.

Cars filled the space outside the motel and two were leaving, as if the drivers had lunched and were now on their way again. It was nearly one-thirty and in spite of her earlier intention to spend more time walking, Kaye was hungry. She lingered in the car park, reluctant to go indoors, and idly surveyed the cars.

Sometimes Ben Hanley came to this place when he was seeing cases in the local hospital and the car on the other side of the path could be his sleek Bentley, but Kaye glanced at the number and knew that it wasn't his. A large American car jutted out from under a weeping willow and she felt a slight shock. It was similar to the one that she had seen Orson Latimer driving when he had the pretty American girl by his side.

She braced herself, wondering if she was hallucinating. First I think that Ben Hanley is here and then I see one American car and just know it belongs to Orson. How stupid can I get? she chided herself. The other two American cars in the park aroused no such feelings and the area was one where many overseas visitors came to climb the hill and exclaim over the pretty scenery.

'I'm getting neurotic,' she said, and made towards the entrance. Inside, she looked about her and wondered if Ercil might be waiting in the bar. It was quite crowded and some people were waiting for seats in the main restaurant.

What had the note said? Table booked in the carvery for one-thirty. That was a relief. If they could be sure of a table, it might save her from instant starvation. Kaye peered round a large man with a bright tie and badly-fitting suit. The tables were all occupied. She tried to see Ercil, but no graceful black woman sat alone. There were three Nigerian students in close conversation but no Ercil.

She turned back and then looked again. A man and a woman sat at one of the far tables, almost hidden by a cheese plant of immense size. The man was looking towards the door as if expecting to see someone he knew, and as Kaye dived back out of sight she knew that it was Orson Latimer. Her mind was in a madness of utter confusion. Orson here, and with a woman who Kaye had never seen at the hospital . . .

She went to Reception and asked if a table had been booked for Miss Ercil Kingston. 'No, madam, I'm afraid not.'

'Anyone from the Princess Beatrice Hospital? Was a booking made for a party?'

'Ah, yes. A table for three. A Dr Latimer rang

and booked for one-thirty.' He looked at the clock on the wall. 'If you are in his party, may I suggest that you take your seat, madam. We *are* rather busy and you should order.'

'No, I am not in the party. There seems to have been a slight misunderstanding. May I use a phone?'

He gestured to the row of pay-telephones at the far end of the bar and she slipped into one of the kiosks, fumbling for change and dialling the number of the hospital. 'Men's Medical, please,' she said as soon as she got through.

'Staff Nurse speaking.'

'Is Sister Kingston there, Nurse? This is Sister Harcourt.'

'I'm sorry, Sister, but she went down to theatre with a man who is having a gastrectomy today and going on to Men's Surgical afterwards. He was very nervous and asked if Sister could go as far as the anaesthetic room with him.'

'Can you tell me when she is off duty?'

'Yes, Sister. She is off tonight and Mrs Hanley is picking her up to take her to a party. She mentioned it just before she left the ward.'

'Thank you, Nurse. No, there's no need to give her a message. She knows our arrangement for tonight.'

Kaye put the phone down and peeped out. There was no sign of Orson Latimer. Kaye slipped out of the building and walked swiftly away into the town. What was he doing now? He had asked Ercil to leave the message for her, knowing that if he asked, there would be no possibility of her going to Box Hill with him. But *why*?

Kaye went into the old inn by the crossroads and ordered a curry and cider. Why ask her to lunch when he already had one woman with him? Did he think it would hurt less if he invited his old love to meet his new lady in the atmosphere of 'We're all civilised people with no hang-ups, aren't we?' Perhaps the over-emotional Roma wanted to have Kaye served up on a dish of humiliation, just to prove that she was old hat, discarded, and she had to believe it . . . honey! No, even Orson wouldn't let that happen, would he?

But the fact remained that he was sitting in a hotel with a good-looking woman who appeared sad rather than sulky and demanding. Perhaps she didn't care for the arrangement, either. Kaye wished that she had taken a closer look. The girl she had seen in the car with Orson was well-dressed and her hair and make-up were immaculate, as if she had all the time she needed to indulge herself.

The woman at the table, however, was not exactly untidy and her clothes were expensive, but her hair was limp and needed a professional cut and shape, her face was pale from lack of make-up or sleep and her eyes were so very sad. Not the type for Orson, surely?

'I'll just have coffee,' she said as the waitress cleared the dishes. She lingered over two cups of very good strong coffee and whiled away the time before meeting Jill and Ercil by looking for lost masterpieces in the many junk shops in the town. She bought a porcelain figure of a child with a face that reminded her of the boy who by now would have smartly flat ears and an impressive pressure bandage to keep them back while the stitches did their job. It was difficult to keep her mind away from the ward, the staff and children—and from the one man who had changed her life and now threatened it once more.

Jill was jubilant. 'Ben is coming down later and we shall have quite a party.'

'Great,' said Kaye, trying to smile. Ercil sat in the back seat as if she wanted to hide in the deep upholstery. 'What happened to *you*?' said Kaye with an innocent expression. She watched Ercil's embarrassment and smiled. 'I looked round the carvery and didn't see you and then discovered that there was no booking in your name or in mine.'

'What did you do?'

'What was there to do? I came away as the place was full and people were lining up for vacant tables. They do a very good curry in the little pub further along the road into the town. I stayed there, looked at the shops and came on here to meet you.'

'Oh!'

'What's the matter? I *am* rather curious to know what that message was all about.'

Kaye was oddly detached at the thought that her very good friend had joined in some conspiracy to make her meet Orson in a situation where she must stay and talk and be civilised. Was that the word she wanted? It didn't matter.

'You didn't see anyone you know?'

'Hardly. But then, I wasn't looking for anyone but you.'

Let her think that it all went wrong. If I don't admit to seeing Orson then they might never know that I had run away. Kaye continued to look blandly innocent and asked Jill if she had remembered to bring the small case containing a change of clothes for the party.

'It's in the boot with mine. I think that our very generous host would like us to stay the night after the party so I put in a couple of nighties in case you and Ercil decide to accept the offer. You have tomorrow morning off, don't you?'

'Yes, but I want to get back and do some shopping and take clothes to the cleaner,' Kaye said.

'And I am on early duty,' said Ercil. 'I'm sorry about the note, Kaye.'

'We all make mistakes,' said Kaye. 'If you decided you couldn't make it for lunch, it doesn't matter. Being in our job makes us adaptable to appointments.' She saw Ercil bite her lip and look as if she wanted to explain that the message had been from Orson, so Kaye said briskly, 'Least said, you know. It hasn't ruined my day and I really didn't care for the atmosphere in the carvery. Forget it.' She patted the other girl's hand and smiled and Ercil smiled uncertainly.

'Not far now,' said Jill. 'Fortunately I came here first with Ben who knew the way, and I think we take this turning.'

She turned the car up into a bumpy lane between hazel hedges and scattered beech saplings, past a ruined barn and the remains of a stone cottage and into a smoother, grass-covered open space. Across the green was a warm stone farm house with huge chimneys and creeper on the walls. A carefully tended central flower bed made a rather alien touch in the general exuberance of plants and Kaye wondered if the whole place would be regimented in time and the appearance ruined by improvement.

'Nice flowers,' said Jill, 'but I think I liked it better as it was. Some people can't leave well alone.'

'I agree,' said Kaye and gave Ercil an old-fashioned look.

Colin Rocco ran out to help them in with their cases. He looked fit and bright-eyed and it was difficult to see in his face the pallor and acute pain he had suffered so few days ago. His father followed more slowly and made the visitors welcome courteously and without the fulsome gratitude that was so unnecessary and slightly embarrassing.

The house was beautiful, with good taste evident everywhere they looked. Muted carpet covered the floors and the corners were lit up with deep bowls of flowers. Antique furniture glowed in the flicker of a log fire that was not needed but added to the charm and drew everyone to its friendly warmth, even on an afternoon in early summer. Colin tugged at Kaye's arm. 'Come and see my pony,' he said.

'Don't be a nuisance, Colin. Make sure he brings you back in half an hour and we'll have tea.' Mr Rocco laughed. 'All right, three-quarters of an hour, but no longer. Sister Harcourt has come down to a party, not to wade through muddy fields.'

'I've already been walking and I can pull off my boots as soon as we come back,' said Kaye. She followed the boy into the field behind the house. In the distance she could hear the hum of a machine and as they cleared the rise, the blades of a reaper beat against the skyline, as it cut the hay. The huge field, made so by the grubbing up of at least four hedges, was impressively rolling up towards the blue sky and the reaping machine was silhouetted as in an etching.

Colin tugged at Kaye's arm and led her to a barn and fenced enclosure with white palings, like a Western corral. New stables with their half-doors open faced them and a horse whinnyed softly. Affluence and good husbandry mixed with the unsentimental destruction of much that was old and picturesque made a cool combination that had to be admired but not loved. But the pony was real and warm, probably uneconomical and somehow comforting. Colin stood on tiptoes to touch the smooth flank and pulled some carrots from his pocket.

The sun was warm on her back and Kaye thought of Vincent. If she married him, she could live in this style, wander out to ride or to gaze at a machine cutting hay and close her eyes under the sun as the scent of new-mown grass came over the fields. It could be a good life and one that Vincent might like as a background against which he could entertain his business colleagues and show off his lovely wife as a precious part of his life and importance. He was rather like Mr Rocco in ambition and the love of possessions.

A lark sang against the sky and she thought of Orson, lying flat on warm grass while another lark shrilled above and made the big American smile with contentment. She smoothed the pony and went along to give a hunter some of the carrots. She breathed deeply and revelled in the pungent odours, the faint smell of hay—and then wrinkled her nose as something more acrid came to her nostrils.

A moment before she had heard a shout but

dismissed it as one man calling to another farm worker trying to make himself heard across a field. But when it came again she started to run to the top of the ridge, suddenly afraid. Colin followed, protesting that he wanted her to look at the rabbits he had been given now that he was better. Kaye stood on the ridge and watched, horrified, as black smoke billowed from the engine of the reaper and enveloped the cab. She couldn't see if the driver was still there or if he had managed to get out before the smoke got to him.

'Run home and tell your father to bring the Land Rover.' She gave Colin a push. 'Don't stand there, Colin. Run!'

She called after him to bring an extinguisher too, and made for the vehicle. The blood in her throat was hot and she gasped as she dragged her feet over the newly-cut grass. The smoke continued to pour out and she could see that the door of the cab was still tightly shut. She forced herself on and round to the other side, gasping for breath, and found a man pulling at the closed door, desperately trying to free whoever sat at the controls. She went to help him and together they heaved in unison, pulling at the jammed door. It gave just as the cab burst into flames and the boy they pulled from the fire held out hands that were encased in burning gloves. The man seized the boy and rolled him in the grass. Kaye tore off her suede jacket and slammed it down on the burning gloves as the grass began to smoulder. There was nothing damp to quell the flames and her jacket had to serve. She watched the fire die and saw the singe marks on the leather, but there was no time for regrets. Kaye took off her scarf and covered the side of the boy's face, where the heat had scorched one cheek, hoping to exclude the air and reduce the shock.

The Land Rover rocketed across the field with the farm manager at the wheel. Mr Rocco jumped out and ran to the cab with a fire extinguisher but had to watch the vehicle burn out as the fuel tank caught and exploded. The farm manager picked up the boy and carried him to the back of the vehicle and Kaye picked up the burned jacket and climbed in beside the boy.

'What the hell was he doing?' demanded Mr Rocco. They drove carefully now, back to the farmhouse where an ambulance was coming up the lane. To her relief, the boy was conscious and less badly injured than she had thought, with only wrist burns and his blistered face.

The ambulancemen transferred him to the comfort of a stretcher and whisked him away to the local hospital. Mr Rocco breathed deeply.

'He crept up when I was having my snack under the hedge,' said the driver of the reaping machine. 'He hung about all morning and I told him to push off and he couldn't have a lift in the cab, but he came back when I wasn't looking. He started up the engine and pulled the door tight. It's very stiff, even for me, and he couldn't open it when the smoke came pouring up at him. I tried, but it took the two of us to get it open, didn't it, miss?'

'Yes, it was a good thing you shouted when you did,' Kaye said. She smiled, trying to bring the atmosphere back to normality. 'Colin was the one who really helped.' The child blushed and relaxed. 'He ran and gave all the right messages, the ambulance was there when it was needed and I think that the boy will be quite all right in a day or so.'

Black smoke still filled the sky above the field and men with water tanks went up to damp down the hay around it in case the fire spread. Kaye put an arm round the child.

'We could see your rabbits now, if you like,' she said. He laughed, released from the memory of near disaster, and his father gave her a glance of gratitude. 'Just five minutes and then I must wash away some of the smoke,' she said, feeling slightly shaky and knowing that her arm was hurting. As the door was flung open, a tongue of flame had burned through the synthetic fabric of her shirt, melting it but not flaming. She put a hand over it and knew that soon she must have it dressed, but now it was important for Colin to forget the seriousness of the accident.

'Later,' said Mr Rocco firmly. He took her hand from the sleeve and drew in his breath sharply. 'You should have gone too.'

'It's nothing. If I could have some salt and water and a dry dressing or fist-aid pad, I'll be fine. It's superficial.'

'Colin, run and tell Sister Kingston to come down, will you?'

'Oh, yes, Ercil will know what to do,' said Kaye and, having convinced herself that there was someone to take over, she swayed and crumpled and never knew that her kind host had to carry her into the house and up to a bedroom.

Dimly, Kaye heard a bustling but orderly movement and felt Ercil's cool hand on her brow. She

heard the rip of her shirt as Ercil cut it from her arm
and winced as warm saline eased the pain of the
burn. Ercil rolled her over and removed the torn
shirt, putting a clean towel under her side to catch
the drips from the irrigation. It was warm in the
heated bedroom and so easy to close her eyes and
let Ercil take the strain.

'I'll have to leave it covered with a dry dressing
until Dr Hanley sees it,' Ercil said.

'It's fine,' said Kaye. 'I'll just rest for five minutes
and then I can come down if you'd help me to
get something over this arm. You're magic,' she
said.

The pain had died back into a dull ache and she
felt warm and sleepy. A bit shocked, she diagnosed, but in a comfortable warm room, not a
bad sensation. The boy would be all right and Mr
Rocco could still have his house-warming. Her lips
twitched. His field was already very warm! She
snuggled down on the top of the duvet with a small
clean towel over her arm and enough towels to mop
up every drop of saline that might have gone on to
the bed.

In ten minutes I'll get up, she promised, and was
surprised to find that she did just that and wandered
out on to the landing, clutching the towel that Ercil
had bandaged lightly over her arm and looking
hopefully for the bathroom.

Below, the front door was flung open and the bell
rang at the same time. Orson Latimer stood in the
hall and looked frantically for someone to answer
him. He held a blackened suede jacket in his hand,
as if it was a poisonous snake that might attack him,
and his eyes were wild.

'Anyone there? For God's sake, tell me what's happening!'

Mr Rocco came out of the sitting-room.

'For crying out, what is happening? I saw an ambulance leaving the lane in a hurry and then I picked up this.' He looked back at the clouds of smoke still billowing from the wreck. 'This is Kaye's coat, isn't it? What have you done to her?'

'It's all right. The boy's fine.'

Orson stared. 'Of course he's all right. He only had a myringotomy. What did you expect?'

'Not Colin. I mean the boy Sister Kaye helped to pull from the reaper when it went up in flames. He went to hospital.'

'And Kaye?' Orson held out the coat. 'Tell me.' His voice was harsh and his eyes dark with pain, and as Kaye stood there watching, the pain in her arm didn't matter any more. He cared enough to be upset that she was hurt.

'She's upstairs.'

Orson didn't wait for more but rushed for the stairs and Kaye went back to her room quietly and pulled the duvet high under her chin, closing her eyes. If she pretended to be asleep, he would go away and calm down and she could remain remote until the bull stopped pawing the ground and looking for trouble. Even his caring now meant trouble. What use would it be if he was good to her now he thought she was injured, when he would be gone tomorrow, to care for someone on a permanent basis?

She heard one door open and shut and a muttered apology as Orson burst in on someone he didn't know. He was still muttering as he came to her door and she tried not to smile. She hadn't heard *that* expression since he left Beattie's two years ago. Maybe it was exclusive to furious Americans.

He stood by the bed and she was conscious of her breathing. Ordinarily she wasn't aware of the intake of breath but now, knowing that he stood over her, she could hear it coming in shallow gasps that were uncontrollable. She fluttered her eyelashes and saw him through the crack.

His golden hair fell forward over stormy eyes. His mouth was hard with some emotion that could have been grief or intense anger. He bent over her and then knelt by the bed and she smelled the male freshness and harshness and his nearness of body and lips and heart. She closed her eyes tightly, trying to fix the faces of the other women in his life firmly in her mind. He was so close that his breath touched her cheek. Then his lips touched her cheek and her lips, her chin and the corner of her mouth where he used to say that love had its home. 'Way deep there, honey, in that dimple, it's all there waiting.'

Her body was floating on a magic carpet of response and the wonder that he was the same and that even if he had a dozen women he could never forget her completely. Her body seemed to melt and she wanted to sigh her love, to groan for a deeper union. His kiss was firmer as he saw her eyes open and he put a hand on her arm. Pain shot up to her shoulder and the throbbing began again.

'Don't!' she cried. 'Please don't.' His pressure increased until she wanted to scream.

'Go away,' she said and pushed his hand from her

arm. She was crying with pain and the inability to explain. He looked at her as if she had cut him with a sharp sword. He sank back on his heels and shook the bright mane of hair as she turned, sobbing, and faced the other way. The loose dressing fell away and he saw the burn. 'Christ, I'm sorry. I was afraid . . . I didn't know I was hurting you.'

He took her hand and now it was not the hand of an old love, or a seducer. 'Stay still,' he said. 'I'll get some dressing. I'll fetch my bag.'

Was it relief in his eyes that let him come back as a doctor? He could care for her professionally and not be personally involved.

Ercil returned with him and he put cool sterile mesh over the burn. The coating of Balsalm of Peru and petroleum jelly made Kaye gasp with pleasure at the relief it brought. Expertly, he bandaged it and Ercil handed him a bright scarf to make into a sling. What had not been said must now remain unsaid. Kaye sat up and tried to laugh.

'Better?' he asked.

'Better. What are you doing here?' She tried to appear unconcerned. 'I thought you were in London.'

'Did you?' The blue eyes were brighter now that the stress had gone. A cynical smile made her drop her gaze. 'I thought I saw you in a certain motel looking for a friend.' She shook her head. 'Strange,' he went on. 'I asked the man at reception if a lovely woman with dark hair was waiting for me and he said that someone had asked about a booking but said she wasn't in my party.'

'Really? Did you have a good lunch?' He *had* seen her as she stood in the doorway looking for

Ercil. 'I suppose the carvery was a good choice. Most Americans like their roast beef, don't they?'

'I wanted to talk to you. I wanted you to meet someone and thought that a restaurant might be a wise choice.'

'I already had my day arranged,' Kaye said quietly. Ercil looked guilty. 'It's all right, Ercil, I know just how persuasive he can be at times. I remember it well.'

Orson picked up his bag and turned to the door. She saw in the set of the wide shoulders the tenseness of anger, the latent strength of a magnificent physique and the sexuality that robbed her of her own strength. She blessed Ercil for being there or she might have cried out for him to come to her, to stay on any conditions, even if it was to meet his new love. His mouth had found the soft droop of her own and the pulse in her white throat and she wanted him as much as she had ever wanted him, with all the darkness of despair and the void of unfulfilled desire.

'I'll get up now,' she said. 'What a good thing I packed an uncrushable caftan that will slip on without difficulty and hide the dressing. It feels fine now and I hope they give us some food soon. I'm starving.'

She hoped it was true or that the others would be convinced of her speedy recovery. She looked out of her window at the last sultry smoke clouds against the sunset, and shivered. Another minute and the boy might have died.

When she went down to join the others for drinks, the buzz of conversation was of one topic only. The boy came from a neighbouring farm and he had a passion for all things with engines. He had already been involved with several minor accidents and could slip into a farm building with all the stealth of a Red Indian tracker.

'The best thing you can do, Rocco, is to get him to work and teach him the right way to do it. Then he won't sneak up and make a goddam mess of himself and others.'

Orson Latimer looked over his glass, eyeing Kaye as if the accident was all her fault. 'Nearly killed a perfectly good hospital sister, and we're going to need her, aren't we?'

Ben Hanley nodded. He came over and asked all the right questions, insisting that Kaye should take time off if she needed it, but even her nice generous Dr Ben Hanley seemed to think that she might go back on duty as they needed her with the new admissions. I'm a very good sister, she told herself as she accepted a glass of sparkling wine. They need me as an efficient machine and machines have no emotions, and if I can keep away from Orson I might be able to stay at Beattie's.

She tried to put space between them but knew that he watched her as she moved about the room, with the floating silk caressing her body in a loose veil, the peacock colours irridescent and beautiful and her hair shining clean and dark.

'I'm sorry if I was stupid not to tell you that he called me,' said Ercil.

'It doesn't matter,' replied Kaye.

'He seemed very anxious to get hold of you and when I told him you were going to Surrey he was upset and said he particularly wanted you to meet someone today.'

'Which of his women was it?' Kaye tried to sound as if it was amusing.

'Roma Sterling. You do know about her?'

'She knows him well enough to give him gold-plated pens and phones him from New York, so I suppose she is a *very* good friend.'

'Oh, you do know. I wasn't sure if it was common knowledge yet. I can't see it remaining a secret if she is in England. Orson asked me not to mention it yet as it might upset certain people who resented outsiders coming here.'

'Like me?'

'No, of course not. Why should you? Some seniors on the staff including Brenda March made murmurings about Americans—but then she would, wouldn't she?'

'She isn't the easiest person I know.'

'You know about the concert?' Ercil laughed and drew her to one side. 'March got some of the tickets and made sure that she had the one next to Orson Latimer. I suppose after the way he had avoided her since his return, it was the last desperate effort.'

'They didn't go there together?'

'No, one of the others said that he was polite but not very friendly and seemed on edge all evening. He swanned off as soon as the concert ended and so March had to go back with Tony in that rattle-trap of his. She wasn't very pleased.'

Kaye smiled wanly. In one part of the concert hall there had been a woman listening to Chopin and thinking not of the man at her side but of another man sitting in the back of the hall. He had listened to the same music; music they both loved and had once shared. What had been his thoughts if he too was sitting with someone he didn't love? He was thinking of Roma, and wishing that she was there, Kaye decided.

Her wine glass was taken from her hand. 'Can I freshen your drink?' Orson looked down at her, and he was just another polite man at a party, doing his duty. 'We eat soon. Did you have any lunch?'

'Yes, I had a very good meal,' she said, 'but I'm quite hungry now.'

'Come and eat,' called Mrs Rocco, and the guests trailed into the dining-room to the magnificent buffet on the long decorated tables. Orson put a hand on Kaye's shoulder.

'Let the lions feed first in case you get hurt in the scrum.'

'I shall be fine.' She slid away from his grasp and walked towards the door, dreading to be alone with him again, dreading his touch and longing for him in love beyond passion. If only she could put her head on his shoulder and weep away her grief and the past bitterness. If only they could put back the years and forget what had come between them; but his opinion of her was firm and could not be reversed. The bull had taken up his stance and knew he was right.

'I must talk to you about a friend who is over from the States.'

'Do you really think I want to hear?' Her voice was unsteady.

'I know you never talk shop off duty, or very seldom, unless I sound off about a case.'

'You call this shop talk? Didn't you say it was about a friend?'

'It's both. She's coming to the Princess Beatrice tomorrow.'

'I see.' Kaye found a plate and let the waiter put cold turkey on it with trimmings and a jacket potato with coleslaw. She took a whole-wheat roll and butter and collected cutlery. At least he was warning her that the woman he wanted would be there, working with him as well as sharing his leisure and his love.

'What is she doing?' he asked, looking across at Ercil.

'She's seen you and is beckoning. You'd better go.' Kaye looked down at her plate and wondered how the food had got there. She had no recollection of being given it and knew she wasn't hungry enough to finish it. She set down the full glass of wine that Orson had brought with him when he followed her to a table and she looked at his plate which staked a claim to the seat by her side. Now Ercil had given him the excuse to free him from the company of an old flame who had to be told about her successor coming to be with him. But he strode back to her and sat down.

'Remind me to make a call,' he said.

'You don't need me. If it's that important, you will remember.'

'I'm still not very good at it.' He grinned and attacked his food.

'It's time you were,' she said. She cut the meat into small pieces and took up her fork, American-style, to eat her food, then saw his amused glance and wished that she had not done so, as it had once been a joke that she couldn't manage to eat with one hand. He had remembered.

'You'll like her,' he said.

'Who?'

'Roma, of course. Ercil said you know about it so I won't spell it out here. Until she gets used to being here and the test is over.'

'A test? I suppose it is,' Kaye said, so softly that he couldn't hear. Women, like old wine, might lose something by travelling from the country of origin, but wasn't it like a man to cold-bloodedly put a woman to a test of suitability?

'I didn't want her to come to England,' he said. 'But she insisted and made a bit of a hassle over it.' He smiled. 'Some women are completely single-minded when it concerns someone they love.'

'So she telephoned you from the States and sent cables?'

'Everything,' he said, and sat back with his wine glass in one hand, relaxed and as if he approved of her tenacity. 'Great little woman, Roma,' he smiled.

'Great,' echoed Kaye. How could he become this fatuous over a hysterical woman, who if she carried on as she was doing after they married, must make life hell for any man? Was she fit to have his love? To have his strong hands caressing her, the deep blue eyes adoring her and his body wakening in desire for her?

'I think I've had enough to eat,' said Kaye.

'You should turn in early. Rocco said to stay the night and I accepted for you.' She opened her mouth to protest and he put a finger on her lips. 'Ben Hanley agrees and told me to stay and keep you in order and dress the burn tomorrow before we go back. That's why I have to telephone and make sure that Roma can cope alone.'

'Please don't stay because of me,' she said stiffly. To be in debt to him was intolerable.

'I like it here,' he said lazily. 'I'm staying for me.'

'It's hot in here. I think I might go out for a while and then go to bed. I can slip away without breaking up the party and you could make my apologies once I know where my case is and where I am to sleep.'

'I know about that. You talk to Ercil and to our hosts and I'll make my call. Ben Hanley will take Ercil back as he has to be in London early tomorrow.'

'Good night,' she said, and left him gazing at her over his glass until she found Mrs Rocco.

'My dear, we were so worried about you. I shall feel so much more happy if you stay here instead of travelling tonight, and Colin will be delighted to have breakfast with you. I know that if he has to go into hospital for anything now, he will never be afraid after all your kindness. Well, I'll show you your room now and you can slip away when you are tired. By the way, we rang the local hospital and there is one very sore but fairly undamaged boy sitting up in bed watching television, so there is no need for any of us to lose sleep over him.'

'That's a relief. I can easily go back tonight, Mrs Rocco. I am fairly unscathed, too.'

'Dr Ben thinks not, and so does that nice American. He seemed very anxious to stay with you.' Mrs Rocco put her head on one side as if inviting confidences. 'He's very attractive. I should think he turns quite a few heads, doesn't he?'

'Quite a few. I think he believes there is safety in

lots of different dates so that no one girl thinks that she is special.'

'How trying. I was firmly convinced that you were the one.'

'I have a boyfriend, as Orson will tell you. He is quite convinced of that fact,' Kaye said. She started.

'How *is* Vincent?' said Orson at her shoulder. 'I can show Kaye her room. Please don't neglect your other guests for us.' He put a hand on Kaye's shoulder and propelled her towards the hall. 'A pity you haven't a hospital cloak with you. Just the thing for wearing over a sore arm.'

'I don't need it.'

'You will. It isn't good to get cold after a shock, as well you know. In the garden it might be chilly.'

'I'm not going out,' she said.

'Chickening out? You pleaded lack of air back there.'

'I'm tired.'

'All the more reason for a burst of oxygen. Get something to put round your shoulders and I'll grab a sweater instead of this jacket.'

'There's no need,' Kaye began, but he opened the door to a pretty room softly lit by rose-shaded lamps and with cream and rose curtains. Her overnight case was by the bed and someone had loosened the straps. Now, it looked as if she was staying for a while.

Orson lingered in the doorway and then went away quickly to his own room. Kaye picked up the cashmere shawl that echoed the colour in her dress in a design of peacock's feathers and frondy grasses. She stared at it and wished she had a sweater or a cardigan that might do instead of the shawl, but as she had come with no real idea of staying overnight, there was nothing suitable that she could pull over the still sore arm.

'You kept it.' A lump in her throat stopped her from speaking. She nodded and looked ahead. Why, of all the garments in her room at the hospital, had she picked up the shawl and added it to the weekend case?

'It's very pretty. A lovely peacock shawl for a beautiful peacock woman.'

She shivered. He had said those words when he bought it for her in an Indian shop when they first planned their trip across Asia. She'd laughed and protested that the female was a peahen, which didn't have the same ring to it. 'You'll have to get used to being male dominated,' he said, and smiled.

'Never. I am me and I do as I choose,' she had said.

'Even if we get married? And that is not a proposal,' he said, teasing her.

'It would cramp your style, wouldn't it?' Already there had been niggling rumours, spread as she now knew by Brenda March, and from the guarded way he referred to her own life when he was not there she guessed he was becoming unsure of her. And it had gone on from there.

He now touched the shawl as they reached the fresh air.

'Are you sure you won't take cold?' She drew away. 'I promise not to touch that arm,' he said and took her hand, tucking it under his warm elbow. A vixen cried over in the copse and as they went past the stables the restless movement of horses added to the remoteness and peace. He turned to her, taking her gently into his arms. 'Kaye, honey,' he said, softly, 'where have you been?'

Her own hunger made her stay, even if it sapped her pride. His mouth was as it had been, soft and questing; his hands sent surges of sweet disquiet through her body and her thighs seemed to weaken, wanting him; and yet there was deep sorrow in her returning kiss. March may have been lying, but some of it was true. He would use her, dominate her until she had no resistance left, just for his own pleasure. How else could he flaunt Roma Sterling as someone he loved? How could he imagine that Kaye would accept another woman in a kind of *ménage-a-trois*?

'We've a lot of sorting to do,' he said.

'I think we have gone past all that.'

'We must.' His lips found hers in a new desperation. 'Kaye, how can I lose you now?'

'You're hurting my arm,' she said, and he knew she was lying.

'We have to talk, but not now. First I must see that Roma is all right and get that settled. After that,' his hand lifted her chin in the pale light and he gazed into the liquid sadness of her eyes. 'After that, we have all the time in the world.'

'Aren't you taking a lot for granted? Do you think you can *settle* a woman and then make love to another? How dumb can you think I am? Brenda March was right. You are nothing but a womaniser. I can't live that kind of life, Orson.'

'What the hell do you mean? I thought I had straightened out Brenda. We had quite a showdown and I don't think you will be troubled by that one again. All that was two years ago and it's no more true now than it was then. Even Vincent . . .'

'What about him? You saw me with him at the concert.'

'Ercil told me that there was nothing in that to menace me.'

'Vincent has asked me to marry him and I haven't said no.' Kaye clutched her shawl closer, a protection against the devil. Good, kind, sensible man who would enfold her with safety and quiet, not threaten her with this aggressive sexuality, this golden strength, this overpowering attraction. She turned and ran back to the house. He had almost convinced her that he still loved her and that this time it was real.

Roma, she repeated in her mind. Roma, Roma. Cling to that name as proof that you must keep your sanity.

She reached the house and went into the welcoming hall, pausing by the table to regain her composure as she could hear voices in the sitting-room. On the pad by the telephone was a message for Orson Latimer. *Roma Sterling rang and will be at the hospital tomorrow at eleven*.

'For you, I think,' she said, pointing to the pad as he entered behind her, and went up to her room.

CHAPTER SEVEN

'ONE NEW baby expected today, Sister, for Maple Syrup urine tests.' The staff nurse closed the report book. 'She was expected this morning but I believe was seen by Dr Hanley at his private surgery first. The mother wanted Dr Latimer to be here when the child is admitted.'

'Very well, Nurse. I'll take over. You've earned a rest.' Sister Harcourt looked down at the book. 'Couldn't the new assistant have coped with the admission and first tests? I believe that Dr Latimer has an addition to his team this morning. Does everything have to wait for him?' she added with a hint of annoyance.

'I haven't heard of anyone new. Tony Smythe was in earlier and so was Dr Charumbera and the X-rays are all here for the next round,' the nurse replied.

Kaye Harcourt gathered her pen and watch from the desk and put them into her top pocket. Her arm was much more stiff than painful, and the expert and impersonal care that Orson had given her after breakfast before driving her back to the hospital in his huge car had made it comfortable. It was no excuse for staying off duty.

They had not talked on the journey. Kaye had sat in the back seat, where she was placed firmly by a solicitous hostess who insisted that she would be more comfortable there. A neighbour who had been a fellow guest at the house-warming had begged a lift to London and had talked all the way there to his captive audience, but at least it had relieved the atmosphere and allowed Kaye to sit back and take no part. Orson had seemed on the point of saying something important but there was never a moment when they were alone from the time they got up and went down to breakfast to the time when he and his passenger had waved her goodbye at the new hostel before Orson politely took the man to his hotel in the heart of London.

Kaye took a deep breath and went out into the ward.

Tony Smythe welcomed her with a wide grin. 'I don't want to set the world on fi-errrr!' he sang out of tune.

'I suppose you've been in cahoots with Ercil this morning?'

'She did mention that you might come back without those lovely long dark eyelashes that drive me mad.'

'Good aren't they, the false ones?' Kaye said smiling, and was very glad to see him.

'You *are* OK?' he asked with a trace of genuine anxiety. 'Just say the word if you need a dressing or an operation or a new arm.'

'I will, but not to you. I'd rather trust my nursing staff,' she said firmly.

'Which one is it?'

'This one, and it's only stiff now.' She picked up a chart. 'I'm back now, so tell me the news. Who have we in bed four and is the side ward clear?'

'I've just been bleeped to ring Dr Latimer,' he said. 'He is on his way now.'

'Big deal,' she said. 'Dr Hanley doesn't expect a fanfare of trumpets each time he enters a ward.'

'Don't be like that. He is bringing up a patient for Dr Hanley. Good paying job, so merits a side ward.'

'We don't take private cases here. What's wrong with the PP wing?'

'The man said . . . And she is going in with two more MSU kids. No difference in treatment, but Dr Hanley insisted that anyone from the States pays if they expect something as important and specialised as this assay and new treatment.'

'I thought he wanted to keep the cases limited to London until he can get clinics formed in some of the provincial hospitals with scientists who are able to cope with this?'

'Is Dr Latimer ever refused anything?' Tony drifted away to check the saline drip at the end of the ward. 'He's getting restless and I think he's had enough, Sister. Dr Hanley said to ask you if you thought he could do without it.' He referred to the patient in the bed and came back with the chart in his hand. 'He's had enough if he is taking by mouth now.'

'Yes, he should be fine. Shall I do it?'

'No, you've some catching up to do. I'll get a dish and that sweet little first year can help me.'

'Hands off. She has a very large boyfriend who boxes.'

'You scare me. I promise not to seduce her in the clinical room,' he smiled.

She was smiling as she turned to the door and Orson thought for one moment that the warmth was intended for him.

'Hi there,' he said. 'I've brought Roma at last.'

Kaye froze. He thinks that I ought to be pleased. How completely insensitive! She stood back to let a woman pass by and saw that this was the one who was with Orson in the carvery. She held the hand of a tiny child who looked up at Kaye with lack-lustre eyes.

'And this is little Sadie, who had been causing a bit of a hassle.'

'Sadie?' Kaye repeated, stupidly. Tony Smythe thrust a chart into her hand.

'Sorry, Sister. I had this and of course you haven't had time to read the notes.' Sadie Sterling, coming to us for MSU testing, the first page said.

She read the rest of them and glanced at the woman with the child. It was all too much to understand, so she gently touched the pale cheek and smiled at the woman with the little girl, who watched her with intense anxiety. She needed attention, that was clear. The child was ill and her mother was worried. That was enough for any nurse to understand and it released the floods of caring and expertise for which the hospital and its staff were famed.

'The side ward, I think,' she said. 'If you would put her to bed while the team get organised, we can get the path people alerted and cut down waiting time.' Orson Latimer might be enamoured of this woman but she needed help.

Kaye led the way to the bright ward where two other children sat watching television. They seemed to lack the normal curiosity of young children. Roma Sterling eyed them with apprehension and looked at her own child, searching for similarities in all of them. Pulling the curtains round the bed, Kaye isolated them and left Roma time to adjust to a strange situation. Tony left to ring the laboratory and Orson studied a letter he had received from Roma's doctor in the States.

'I'm glad you've seen sense,' he said. 'I didn't believe that you could be so prejudiced as to refuse care to a child just because she wasn't first in line for assessment.'

'I never said I was.'

'No, but you grew hackless each time I tried to talk about it and wouldn't meet with Roma.'

Kaye stared at him, unable to find an excuse that would not show him at once that she had thought Roma was a hysterical woman afraid to let the man she loved out of her sight for five minutes. How was she to know that the phone calls, the cables, the frantic pleading, was the fierce desire of a woman for her child?

'I was talking to Millie and she tried to explain. It's only natural that you should be up-tight about favours to friends of staff—she understands because so many people ring her to try and get seats with the airline for which she works.'

'Who is Millie? Not another American with MSU? It would be nice to be told something about my own ward.'

He laughed. 'You have yourself to blame—and Ercil told me you were in the picture.'

'A slight case of crossed lines,' Kaye said, and hoped fervently that he would not pursue the matter. 'And Millie?'

'Ah, Millie is a very good friend. She is a lovely

lady who works for an airline and looks me up if she knows I'm in Boston or London.' Kaye recalled the well-dressed woman in the car. So they had seen her and talked about her seemingly bloody-mindedness.

'She sounds like someone for confiding all your problems to. Do you talk about your colleagues all the time?'

'Not all the time,' he said calmly. 'We have fun, too.' He touched her hand. 'How is the arm?'

Kaye flexed her fingers. 'Stiff when I do that, but getting better all the time,' she said.

His touch was more traumatic than any left-over pain from the burn. Nothing has changed. Even if he isn't in love with Roma—and there was still that possibility, or why should he take so much trouble over a patient or an acquaintance—he was dating women and there was no reason to suppose he wanted his life to run on other lines.

The medical scientist arrived to take specimens and to start the assay, charting the findings so that treatment could be commenced as soon as possible. The recovery of the first children tested was steady and very encouraging. They had begun to emerge from their apathy or attacks of nervous aggressive-ness and their dwindling intelligence. Fits were few after the treatment started and one of the earlier and bad cases now did puzzles and laughed more than at any time during her short life.

Kaye turned her attention to the other children on the ward and hoped that Orson would be so busy with the series that he would have no time to notice her.

'Michael,' she said, with a delighted smile. 'What

a handsome man you are going to be!' The boy's ears were well-shaped and moulded close to his head and the fine line of healing scar was the only sign that he had been to the operating theatre. He held up a mirror and looked at himself complacently, fully conscious of the difference in his appearance.

'Is the telly man coming back?' he said.

'I don't think so. You were on the last film quite a lot, so don't be greedy,' she said.

'But that was before I had my new ears. I don't want everybody to see me like that. Can't they come back and take a picture now so I can show them at school?'

'Sure, that can be arranged.' Orson Latimer leaned on the bed-end and squinted along the bed at Michael. 'It won't be television but I can take a picture for you to show around.' He frowned in mock disapproval. 'And shouldn't you be in the day room?'

'He can't take his mirror in there in case it gets broken,' said Kaye. 'I wonder if we did right in improving his image? He's so vain that when he gets to school he might have an even worse time than when they all called him Dumbo.'

'Promise?' said Michael and put the mirror away on his bed-table.

'Promise.'

'It had better be soon, then,' said Kaye. 'Michael goes out tomorrow if the stitches are ready for removal. Dr Hanley said that he can go in any case as the spray will protect them long enough for him to come up to Out-patients.'

'Right, I'll get my camera.'

Kaye watched Orson walk as far as the day room with the small boy. He looked good with children, but then he always had looked good.

She tidied the rumpled cover on Michael's bed. Everyone had the right to live life in any way he chose and if casual indulgence in sex and brittle relationships were what he wanted, she had no right to object as there was no longer any bond between them. She picked up a toy dog that had fallen from the next cot and bent to speak to the infant who regarded her with wide brown eyes and a solemn expression.

Cilla was waiting for an examination and looked listless and hot. Kaye glanced at her chart and saw that her temperature had shot up since last night when she was admitted. She had drawn her knees up in bed and seemed to be more comfortable in the curled-up foetal position. Kaye took the tiny wrist and found a very febrile pulse. It was so much faster and more thready than the earlier one that she wondered if some mistake had been made in charting it. She bleeped Tony Smythe who was just leaving.

'Couldn't bear to see me go, Sister?' he joked, but came quickly to the cot. 'She's due to be seen by the surgical registrar as soon as his list is over. She's OK according to the last round. What's the rush?'

Kaye showed him the chart and Cilla's latest pulse rate. 'I haven't disturbed her to take her temperature, but you can see that her respirations are rapid and shallow and the pulse speaks for itself.'

He bent to put a couple of fingers on the pulse at

her temple and whistled softly. 'How right you are. The pulse is almost uncountable.'

'Is the list over?'

'You're right, she ought to be done now. They did make a positive diagnosis of appendicitis, so that much is clear.' He went quickly to the house telephone and asked for the theatre sister concerned, and when he came back he was frowning. 'The surgical registrar left the house surgeon to stitch the last case and had to get down to one of the sector clinics to see an emergency. Sister says the theatre can cope now if we can find a surgeon.'

'I thought I saw Mr Dealware go into Men's Med some time ago to see the gastric case that Ercil is transferring to surgical as he hasn't responded to diet.' She bit her lip. 'I can't think he would do—he never operates on children.'

'Where's our budding film star?' said Orson, waving an impressive Polaroid camera.

'That can wait,' said Kaye. 'We are worried about Cilla.'

'Temperature?'

'I haven't taken it as she isn't very happy, but she's very hot and her pulse is terrible. It's shot up very suddenly.'

Orson glanced at the chart and then at the pinched little face, grey-dark on the pillow. 'What are we waiting for?' he said. 'Get moving, Tony.'

'We haven't a surgeon. I'll buzz the office and see who is in the building. The theatre is at the end of the list and only the house surgeon is still there, stitching the skin and doing the notes.'

'I'll do it.' Orson looked more closely at the chart. 'She's really sick, this one.' He looked at

Kaye with approval. 'You sure have the touch, Sister. It's often difficult to know when a black child is ill as their faces don't show the usual pallor, but I know all about it from experience. Ring the Theatre Sister and tell her to hang on to the anaesthetist for a query perforated appendix and stomach aspiration to get rid of her breakfast.'

'I don't think she ate anything, but she was drinking a lot of squash earlier. I'll tell them.'

'Sister?'

Kaye looked up sharply. She was bending over the cot side, putting the soft toy into the child's arms for comfort, the curve of her breast accentuated by her posture and on her face an expression of sweet compassion. She saw the flash of the camera and the suddenly tense smile as Orson took the picture. He swung away to the corridor and she knew that she was blushing.

Glimpses of the man she had once known, small moments of recall that told of other days, other photographs, made her heart beat faster. She remembered that he had a video tape of the television documentary in the ward and he could freeze her picture as often as he liked, watch her holding a child in her arms. Was she to be one of his picture gallery? Had he a book in which he put photographs of old flames?

She stayed with Cilla while the nurse dressed her in a tiny white gown and socks and she placed a small soft towel under her head on the trolley pillow when the porter came.

'Sister?' She turned to her staff nurse. 'Mrs Sterling is asking for Dr Latimer. She wants to stay with Sadie for a while but the Path people would really like to take tests without her being there as she makes the child very nervous.'

'I'll see her,' said Sister Harcourt. She braced her shoulders and for some reason her burned arm seemed heavy and stiff, as if trying to hold her back from doing something she didn't want to do. She opened the door to the side ward and smiled at Elizabeth, the medical scientist, who looked slightly annoyed. Roma Sterling sat on the end of Sadie's bed and stared at her as she came into the room.

'Could you spare a moment, Mrs Sterling? I'd like to talk to you in my office.' She glanced at her watch. 'It has to be now, I'm afraid, as I have a busy day. I can show you some of the results we've had over the past year and I hope it will show you what can be done.'

Kaye turned away, confident that the woman must follow; she heard her call, but didn't look back. She went to her office and took out the notes of three children who had shown a dramatic improvement when their diet had been adjusted to cut down the amino-acid imbalance. A minute later Roma Sterling appeared, looking resentful. Kaye smiled calmly and shut the door.

'Good. I can spare you ten minutes now and then I suggest that you go to your room and rest. Sadie can play with toys and have a nap too. Both of you must be very tired and a bit overwrought.'

Roma Sterling tightened her lips. 'Where is Orson?'

'Dr Latimer is in the operating theatre dealing with an emergency.'

'And I suppose that Sadie isn't?'

'Don't you think you could relax, Mrs Sterling? From what I hear, you moved heaven and earth to get Beattie's to accept Sadie for treatment and she is here, safe and in good hands. The sooner the tests are done, the sooner an assessment can be made and the screening begun. You came here because we can help you, so why not let it be so?'

Roma Sterling passed a tired hand over her hair.

'You're so very tired,' said Kaye gently. 'You must have been worried out of your mind when you thought that Sadie might be mentally sub-normal, but take a look at these charts and these before and after pictures.'

So that was why Orson had a camera so handy when Michael asked him. He was taking pictures of the new admissions for the record.

Roma Sterling gazed at the last picture of a happy, wickedly mischievous face that laughed up at the camera, and she burst into tears. Kaye went to the door and asked the junior nurse to bring coffee and biscuits to the office. Roma Sterling shook with deep tearing sobs and her lank hair fell about her face in damp strings of unloveliness. Her nose was red and she scrubbed at her tears with a used handkerchief. Kaye handed her a box of tissues that were very useful for mopping up of many kinds in moments of stress. She waited until the stormy sobs died into a series of hiccups. The coffee arrived just at the right moment.

'I'm sorry,' muttered Roma Sterling. 'I guess everything got on top of me.'

'Of course it did. Now, I believe that you have one of the visitors' rooms? When you've had coffee, go and unpack.' Kaye smiled. 'I bet you haven't even opened your case.' Roma managed a small lift of her lips that could have begun a smile. 'Unpack and take a bath and sleep for a while. I'll send someone to call you and you can come and read to Sadie later and tuck her up for the night. Don't go back now. It's only fair to her to leave her to get used to the other children before she has to sleep there.'

'She could stay with me. She isn't a bed case.' The resentment was returning.

'You are right. There is no need for her to be in bed except when we need her to be for her tests, but the main part of the screening is observation of all she does and is able to do, her reactions to certain things and so on. If she is in a controlled environment we can supervise her diet and her activity.' Kaye smiled with encouragement.

'You are an intelligent woman but there are some who might ruin her treatment by giving her food that is poison to her body and mind. Even in the general ward, she might be given sweets and goodies brought in by other mothers and shared generously by the children. I promise that if she needs you I'll give you a call.'

'I'd like to see Orson before I go over.'

'You can't.' The firmness in the Sister's voice made Roma Sterling look away. 'If you want results, you must trust us and there are many other children needing more urgent attention. Go and sleep, and tomorrow you can help us here.'

'I can?' she brightened. 'Really?'

'There are many ways you can help. The children in the day room break toys and we need at least three large teddy bears to be sewn up again. That would be a great help as the nurses haven't time for sewing.' Roma stood up, swaying with exhaustion. 'Get some sleep,' repeated Kaye gently. 'It will all look better when you are rested.'

'Now I know what Orson means,' said Roma Sterling. 'He's a great guy and the best cousin a woman ever had. I give him hell from time to time, but he never failed me once since Newton died. I just love that man, don't you?'

'He's a very good doctor,' said Kaye.

'Right . . . he's that too.' She picked up her bag. 'Hell, I look awful. My hair!' She ran a hand through the lank and too-long hair. 'Thanks a lot, Sister. What did you say your name was?'

'I don't think I did. I'm Kaye Harcourt.'

Roma stared at her. Kaye could feel the deep appraisal and wished that the woman would go away. She no longer looked resentful but curious and rather amused.

'Kaye Harcourt. Well, that follows,' she said. 'See you later, Sister Kaye. I heard a lot about you from Orson's air stewardess who saw me across London and coped with Sadie while I met with Orson.' She laughed. 'She did it as a favour for services rendered, I believe.'

Kaye sat quite still after she left. She could never like Roma Sterling, even if she wasn't sexually involved with Orson. She was too demanding, too selfish and bossy—or would be, given the chance, she thought grimly. They were cousins and that gave her some extra influence with the handsome and kind doctor, but there could still be a deeper involvement. She had spoken of the pretty stewardess with slight scorn, as if she was just one of many of Orson's girlfriends, or even a rival, but she had been glad to use her as she would use anyone she thought might be of value in some way.

Kaye went back to the ward. She had almost prayed that if Orson Latimer could be saved from the clutches of Brenda March, he could have the American. But was she any better bargain? I'm just jealous and hateful, she decided. If only he had never come back, life could be good here.

Michael came rushing from the day room, brandishing a picture. 'He sent it down as soon as he fixed it.'

The Polaroid picture showed Michael standing up very straight in a very long dressing-gown. He was grinning and showing the gap in his front teeth, which didn't bother him at all. The ears sat back and looked good.

'He did it before he ran up the stairs and said he'd send it down.'

Kaye smiled. Orson might have grave faults where women were concerned, but she had never known him to break a promise to a child, however busy he was.

'He's got a smashing one of you, Sister.'

'The one with Cilla.'

'No, not with her. You don't want to be taken with her. She yells all night.'

'That's the only one he took.'

'This one isn't that.' And with that logic, Kaye had to be satisfied. But it was a creepy feeling, like being on Candid Camera, when she had no idea of being snapped.

The day wore on with two children going home and two more taking their places. Cilla came back into the end cot with its plethora of monitors and respiratory aids. The tiny chest lifted and fell convulsively and the small naked body in the ventilator fought for survival with the help of a drip and antibiotics. Orson came to the ward briefly to check on her post-operative condition and Kaye sensed his anxiety.

'Was it perforated?'

'Yeah.' His voice was flat. 'We didn't have all the picture. The mother thought she had colic and gave her a dose which made everything worse. She'd had two attacks at home before this one, but they said at first that this was the only one, so she was ready to pop—and she did.'

He examined the small drainage tube sewn into the wound. 'Had to do that, but I don't like it. She needs to be held up as soon as she is over the gas. It can't drain at that angle but she needs to be flat for her circulation just now. If she responds, she could come out in a few hours. The trouble is that she has been given antibiotics before she came in and we don't know what they were. If she is resistant to them, we might have struck lucky with our choice or we might not.'

'I'll keep a half-hourly chart and cuddle her as soon as she can be held.'

'You're good at that. Very comforting, a cuddle from Sister Kaye.' She blushed.

'Lots of practice and all a part of the job,' she said.

'Guess you've progressed a lot. How far now? Qualified to cuddle high-powered industrialists, I believe.' He laughed. 'Don't get mad at me. I forgot to give you a message. Brenda March asked to tell you that Vincent rang and wanted you to ring back as soon as possible.'

'Why did March tell you that?' she said, as if she couldn't guess.

'Why, indeed? You all know how I forget things, but at least I've given it now.'

'When was this?'

He looked up at the ceiling. 'I reckon he rang last night and she told me this morning when I was coming over.'

'Thanks a lot for the speedy delivery,' Kaye said caustically.

'Think nothing of it,' he said generously. 'Tell me, do I get invited to the wedding?'

'No,' she said. 'And talking of bossy women like March, your cousin was asking for you. I sent her to rest and bath and get settled while the path people took specimens. She was getting in the way.'

'Just one of her less lovable habits,' he said, moving off. He came back. 'How did you manage it? She swore she wouldn't leave Sadie for a minute and I couldn't move her.'

'Charm and nerves of steel,' Kaye said lightly. 'And this *is* my ward.'

'I have something for you. Show it to Cilla's mum when she visits, but I want it back.' He handed her the photo he had taken of her cradling the little girl.

'Good enough for *Picture Post*,' Kaye commented.

'*Picture Post* is no more.'

'I know,' she said, and put it in the pocket of her dress, trying not to let him see how much she liked it. 'What about the other snaps? Michael told me you had more.'

'Oh, those.' He walked away, and she couldn't ask him more as one of the fracture children wanted her to rub an itch where he couldn't reach it. When she was free again, he was in the side ward with Ben Hanley.

A junior nurse came to her, bursting with importance. Three weeks out of her first block, she was keen to show her interest in everything. Sister Harcourt smiled, knowing that the girl had helped collect specimens of urine for testing.

'Sister, I took some urine from one of the children in the side ward and put it in the specimen jar as you told me, but it does smell funny.' She wrinkled her nose as if trying to recapture the smell. 'Like something sweet,' she said. 'I don't think she could have dropped something in the bedpan without me seeing, but should I take another specimen when she can produce one?'

'No, Nurse. That's very observant. She is in here because her urine smells like maple syrup and it has a cause.' Kaye smiled. 'Ask Dr Smythe when he has the time to tell you. He knows all about it and you missed the talk that Dr Latimer gave here a few nights ago.'

The new nurse blushed, and Kaye knew that Tony was already running after her with his usual zeal. 'But don't waste too much time with him. You do have ward work to do, Nurse.'

Kaye went on her round, thinking back to the early days of training when the least attractive of the medical students and doctors had at least an aura of potential greatness. Anything in a white coat made the heart beat a little faster, until one man came out of the blue with all the taurean arrogance and sexuality of a strange god, a man who changed her life and filled her mind and dreams with thoughts of love and marriage and everlasting fidelity. She recalled Vincent and sighed. There was time to ring him now that the ward was quiet, but her hand hovered over the telephone and she couldn't think what to say, even if she got through to him. His message might now have no meaning as it had been given her so late.

She tidied her desk and checked the next medicine list. I'll ring tonight, she thought, unable to overcome the guilty sensation she still had whenever she made a private call while on duty.

'Ah, there you are, Sister Kaye.' Ben Hanley smiled from the doorway. 'Sadie is going to be fine. Thank God for fussy mothers who see danger before it comes. We can catch this at once and she'll have to come over every six months for screening and stabilising, but she can be sure of a good future.'

'Her mother will be very pleased,' said Kaye.

'And what about you? Has anyone looked at your dressing today?'

'I did it this morning, but it was too weepy to spray. I'll take another look tonight,' said Orson Latimer. Kaye regarded the two men. 'She left it to blister instead of dousing it with saline, and there is a patch of skin that ought to go,' said Orson.

'I now know how patients feel whenever you do a round and discuss them over the beds. To you we are just bodies!'

'It depends on the body,' said Orson with an insolent smile. 'But you'd better let me see that burn again.'

'I thought I'd go along to Ercil. She can dress it for me.'

'She's off duty tonight. I'll be along after you've given report to the night staff. Have a tray ready.'

'There's no need, and I think you have many other calls on your time. Mrs Sterling was asking for you again earlier. Somehow she has the number of the ward and rang through on the house phone.'

Orson frowned. 'That was naughty. She was told not to do that.' He sighed. 'I've had my cousin up to the eyebrows for a while. I know she was worried, but she's like a leech.'

'You should be flattered. All men with large egos like their women to cling, don't they?'

Ben Hanley laughed and left them alone. 'Don't let Sister Kaye get out of having her arm dressed by making you mad, Orson,' he warned.

'I like my women to know I'm around,' Orson said. 'I also like them loving and pretty and available.'

'And various,' she said. 'How is your pretty stewardess?'

'Fine, I think, but far away in Tokyo.'

'So you have to look elsewhere for feminine company?'

'Not very far. I was about to ask you to come and look at my pictures tonight.'

'I have to make a phone call,' she said. 'I'll have a dressing tray ready first and you can have some coffee on the ward.'

'With you all starched and on duty, sitting way off across the room.' His eyes were wary and full of veiled anguish.

'Yes, Orson,' she said firmly. 'I like to date one

man at a time. I have always felt like that, whatever
you might think of me.'

'You are going to ring Vincent?' She nodded. He
caught up his stethoscope and swung it to and fro
until it hit the desk and came away from the tubing.
'Hell,' he said, picking up the pieces and fixing
them again. 'Why him? You can't marry that
smooth lizard.'

'Vincent, a lizard?' She laughed, almost natur-
ally. 'Really, Orson!' She picked up the house
phone to answer the buzz and turned away as if
dismissing him. The dispenser was querying an
order and she had to look up the chart and the
prescription to sort out Tony Smythe's handwriting. Orson gave a growl of discontent and left her to
her work. He looked like a boy who had been
refused a toffee-apple. It should have been a small
victory for her, but when she was alone and quiet,
she felt weak and lost and very sorry for herself.

CHAPTER EIGHT

NURSE BENSON put her head round the door. 'Oh, I'm sorry, Sister. I can see you can't come to the phone. Can I take a message? Mr Burgess is on the phone.'

Kaye Harcourt glanced up at the stern face of the doctor irrigating her burn. He gave no sign of letting her drip her way to the telephone in the office only a few yards away.

'Tell him I'll ring when I can but I am still on duty,' said Kaye.

'No, Nurse. Tell him that Sister Harcourt will not be free this evening as she has burned her arm. She is having it dressed and then will be resting as she is very tired.'

'I'm not. Ouch!' Kaye twisted her arm as if to free it from his grasp and the taut skin stretched.

'You see, Nurse? Give the message please.' He gave her a charming smile that included her in his scheme for protecting Sister Kaye from her own folly. 'Tell him that Sister will ring sometime tomorrow.'

'Yes, Dr Latimer.'

'And Nurse Benson, it's good to know that you are now in charge on night duty here.'

The girl blushed deep red and ran back to the office.

'My friend for life,' said Orson Latimer complacently. 'But she is a very good nurse. I like to

175

give credit, don't you, Sister?'

'To think that you called Vincent a lizard! You are the smoothest of smoothies and now I suppose that girl will dream of you.'

'I could do with some dreams,' he said. 'Mind if I join yours?'

'You left mine a long time ago,' Kaye said. He took a pair of very fine scissors and cut away the puckered skin that surrounded the burn and with it the last of the melted synthetic fibres clinging to the area.

Kaye was aware of his gentleness and her heart was heavy. His touch was healing and his skill could help and save, but his heart and body could never be hers. He ran more warm saline over the red patch; now all the blistering was gone and it was clean. He cut a neat patch of Tulle Gras to cover the red and lowered it gently into position. 'A pity you can't spray it and leave it,' she said.

'It was deeper than you thought and will have to granulate up a little. A spray at this stage would only make it pucker and drag and ruin the line of that lovely arm.' She tried to draw away. 'Hold still, woman. I'll strap it, with airholes to stop it getting soggy, but you'll have to keep it out of the shower.'

His finger traced the line of the soft flesh to the elbow and caressed the bend that was warm and soft as a dimple.

'Please, Orson . . .'

'With pleasure,' he said, and bent to kiss her lightly on the mouth. She shook her head. 'Sorry,' he murmured, but his eyes were bright. 'Sorry I made your uniform wet but you did wriggle. Better change as soon as you can before you ruin my good dressing.' She glanced at him sharply but his face was innocent. What he said made sense, but she couldn't lose the suspicion that something devious was cooking in his fine golden head.

'What about coffee? I had it ready in the office.'

'Coffee?' he said with a delighted smile as if he had been invited to a royal garden party. 'Now that sure would hit the spot. We'll have some in the house yonder. Not in my room, if that bothers you, and not in yours. The music room is often empty among this bunch of Philistines and the chairs are good. I think they rescued them from the old place. Remember them? Deep and soft and cosy and big enough for two?'

'Don't. I ought to ring Vincent.' If she could cling to that, she would be safe.

'Not big enough for three. Sorry, but that's too much.'

'Fool,' Kaye said, beginning to laugh.

'Better,' he said. 'I thought you'd lost that laugh. Where's it been?'

'I'll go and change and make coffee,' she replied.

'We could go out somewhere?'

'After telling Vincent that I had to rest? Really, Doctor, you should be consistent.'

'Ten minutes,' he conceded. 'And I've had no dinner. Thank God the guest rooms for relatives of patients are not in the hostel. We can sneak past Roma.'

'She's probably asleep. She really is very tired and once her anxiety has lightened she will sleep the clock round.'

'True. I admire your sense of fairness, Kaye.

You don't like her but you make excuses for her,'
Orson said softly.

'Very British,' said Kaye dryly. 'And I don't have
to meet her socially.'

'You can't avoid it. You'll see her when you go to
the States. I have to go back with some notes and
read a paper about these cases and you have to have
a pinch graft to that burn if you want to look
beautiful again.'

'I can wear long sleeves and in time it will be
hardly noticeable.'

They went down in the lift and Kaye was glad
that they had for company one porter and a trolley
loaded with sterile drums, even if he was using
the wrong lift for it. Orson looked less indul-
gent, but Kaye spoke to the man and asked after
his wife who had recently had a hysterectomy
at the same time that her little boy was admitted
with an infected neck gland, and Orson remained
silent.

The night air met them, distilling the warm smell
of polish and hospital corridors and bringing a hint
of blossom across from the park.

'It's too late for the magnolia, and too early for
roses,' he said. 'I suppose that all the young things
go across the park under the weeping willows and
the magnolias. Have the bushes at the back finished
flowering?'

'There are some left, if you mean the rhododendrons and the cherry.' Kaye pointed them
out.

'Do they still find big leaves and wrap them
around blossoms to give to their loves?'

'Don't, Orson, it isn't fair.'

'You, who I found so fair . . . touch of your lips, smell of your hair . . .'

'Not that sort of fair,' she said, trembling. 'My arm is getting cold. I have to get inside fast.'

'Of course,' he said. 'Do you need any help undressing?' He ducked away from her anger. 'Forget it. I only wanted to help. Just professional.' But he laughed in the throaty way he had when elated. 'Get changed and if you aren't down here in five, I'll get you.'

So there was to be no escape. He was at a loose end with the pretty stewardess away and Roma too tired to amuse him. Kaye knew that he had not dated anyone at Beattie's since his return—unless she counted the forced encounter with Brenda March at the concert.

She struggled out of her dress and found the loose caftan that she had worn at the house-warming. The gentle folds were soothing and pretty. She brushed her hair out and wondered if it would look more severe pinned up in a French pleat as she wore it on duty, but knew that this would show her fear. She added a reckless amount of lipstick and pale amber eyeshadow and wondered why she looked good.

The telephone rang as she went downstairs but it stopped quickly. She breathed deeply. It was becoming more and more difficult to think of Vincent with any pleasure.

Did everyone go after what might be of use to them? Vincent loved her in his way, but she was of use to him and this would influence him when it came to asking her to marry him. She was a great success with his friends and would run his home

well, bear him pretty children and make the picture
of an influential and prosperous man complete.

Orson loved her still, after a fashion, and wanted
her body to satisfy the needs of a healthy male
animal. No, that wasn't fair. He was intelligent and
skilled, gentle and caring for those who needed
help. She recalled his deft fingers dressing her arm.
It was liquid sunlight that he filtered on to her
injury, that made everything devoid of pain except
her heart, which burned as her arm would never do.
He was wonderful, a devil and if he wanted to make
her remember the old days, he had only to mention
the park, the magnolia trees or any tiny moment
they shared to bring her trembling within her shell
of bright protection built up over the past two
years.

He was in the kitchen with a tray of coffee and
rolls stuffed with Brie and salad.

'You didn't eat either,' he said and went into the
small music room. 'Did you bring the fruit?'

She nodded and placed the dish on the table.
How stupid. She had brought it down today just as
she had done in the past, each time they ate in the
sitting-room or in the medical school, with Orson
bringing some food and Kaye bringing fruit and
cake.

'Not that old thing?' he crowed. 'Couldn't you
get anyone to break it?' She gulped and unwrapped
the chocolate sponge cake, waiting for him to say
that it was his favourite and to grab a piece before
he ate his cheese. He put down the ugly bowl they
had bought one morning when they went to Petti-
coat Lane and Kaye thought she was bidding for a
vase, only to find this monstrosity wrapped in the

lurid pink tissue when she got it home.

'It is very useful,' she said, wishing that she had thrown it out long ago. She cut the cake and he took a slice and munched ecstatically. 'That, at least, is not the same,' she said.

'Better. I like the filling.'

She smiled and poured coffee and he lifted the lid on the box of cassettes by the player with the hand he wasn't using for cake. 'Remember this? For crying out, this is mine! I taped it and wrote the titles on it. I must have left it behind.'

He slid it into the player and sat back eating the roll and cheese. She took a deep breath when she found the tune was not one that had shared memories, and began to eat the fresh food. 'When you come over to the States,' he said, when the dated pop music stopped.

'I'm not going there as far as I know,' said Kaye quickly.

'You have to get that scar fixed.'

'For heaven's sake, aren't there enough surgeons here to do that?'

'I have a friend who is an artist with plastic surgery,' he said.

'I don't need plastic surgery. I suppose he does nose jobs and false boobs and face-lifts, too. What else do you suggest to make my trip worth while?'

'He'd do it well as a favour to me. He owes me and I owe him, so we trade skills.'

'What did he do for you? My, is that why you look so young, Dr Latimer?'

'He mended the face of a very pretty girl who got caught in an accident on a runway when she was leaving an aircraft in a snow storm. A truck skidded and she dived to get someone out of the way and caught it.'

He picked out the biggest apple from the dish and polished it on his shirt. 'She came in to us for the fractures. I was on bones then.' He grinned. 'Brenda March thought I was taking the bones job here. I hope she hates orthopaedics. She's got them for good now.'

'And the girl?' Kaye went back to the time when she was waiting for a bus and Orson drove by with a very pretty woman with a bright, happy smile.

'You saw her once, even if you tried to look as if you hadn't seen us. Looks good, doesn't she? You should see the first pictures we took. I asked Rob to treat her and he did miracles.' He laughed. 'It was almost a repeat of that ballet when the doll is given life. He fell for his own handiwork, I keep telling him. He tells her that he only married her to keep his records intact. He couldn't have some other man claiming she was all his own work, could he?'

'He married her?'

'And I was witness at their wedding. Great couple. You'll like them.'

'I'll take your word for it, but I have no plans to visit America.'

'No need. He's coming over to stay while she has leave in the UK. He can see your arm at the same time.'

'There's no need. I can have it done here.'

'Sure you can.' He shrugged. 'You can let it ride for good and be self-conscious on every beach when you go topless.'

'That would really make me self-conscious, not one small scar.'

'Pity,' he said with a lazy smile. 'You have all the potential, Sister Kaye.'

She got out of her chair and poured more coffee, handing him the basket of fruit, but he took more cake. 'You'll put on weight,' she said.

'Only the woman who marries me is allowed to say such things,' he said.

'I'm sorry. What shall I play? Brahms? The Beatles or Leonard Cohen? That's really old. Not very uplifting.' She pushed the tape aside, knowing that if she played it she would cry.

'You loved it once.'

'I did? It must have been a century ago.'

'Let's have the Beatles. Such nice boys, as my mother used to say in their heyday. Such clean-looking boys and quite good music.' Kaye smiled and put the tape in the slot and sat down in a small Victorian chair with a high back that made her look dignified and aloof. She nibbled some grapes and put the pips into an ashtray.

Orson watched her closely. She wished that she had chosen another chair. There was no way she could slide down and turn away, making it impossible for him to see her face. The music started and everything was fine until they came to 'Eleanor Rigby'. *All the lonely people* . . . She knew why he watched her so closely.

'It's a bad tape,' she said.

'Leave it,' he commanded. 'Remember the night of the fog? Remember the night we were lost and could hear sounds and see shapes but no way home?'

'Don't. I hate fog.'

'We found that café and sat drinking bad coffee

for hours until it lifted and we found the underground. All the lonely people were there that night,
remember?'

'No, I don't,' she flared. 'It's all gone, Orson, and
you can't bring it back and expect to take over
again.'

He put down the coffee-cup. 'Vincent rang
again. For some reason he didn't believe the message, as Nurse Benson thought she would impress
him by mentioning my name as your medical consultant. Seems as if he doesn't like me much.'

'When did he ring?'

'Just before you came down.' Orson grinned. 'I
think he was in one hell of a state. I send him
messages and then I am the one who answers the
phone when he rings you. He wasn't very polite.'

'What happened? Did he ask me to ring him at
home?' She started up and made for the door.
'What did he say?'

'He wanted you to go over and sweet-talk a
client.'

'I don't believe you. If he knew I was hurt, he'd
be very concerned.'

'He thinks that I made it up and, as he said, your
French is so much better than his and you'd like
these people. He said he'd call for you in half an
hour and to be ready.'

'He wouldn't! Orson, tell me the truth. He isn't
like that. I'm going to ring his home.'

'He isn't there. He is in the plush lounge of a
hotel waiting for you. You have a little time yet
before you need to go.'

'I don't understand. You said he was sending a
car for me. Vincent never lets me go anywhere

alone at night. He's much too considerate.' She let her hands fall to her sides. 'What *did* happen? What am I to believe?'

'Believe what you like. Believe what you want to believe.' He took the tape from the machine and looked for another as if she had already left the room. 'I said that when you were ready, I'd put you in a taxi. He was quite pleased with me. Seemed to think he'd won a prize or something. Very smug is our Vincent.'

'He's not.' Kaye paused at the door, knowing that she didn't want to get in touch with him, and she thought back to many dates made quickly because Vincent needed her as a hostess. They had been fun most of the time, but sometimes boring. The men talked shop about money and business and their women-folk never seemed on her wavelength. I never want to hear about another deep freeze as long as I live, she had said one night to Ercil after a long session over rich food and too much wine.

'He understands that after a busy day you need time to pretty-up. He can wait for a while but he wants you there all sparkling, as if nurses never did anything of importance and can wait on their men with smiles like grinning geisha girls.'

'Stop it! It isn't like that. It couldn't be. He needs me. He's the only man who ever did need me,' she protested.

'I need you, Kaye.' She turned and his broad shoulders almost hid the lamp on the table, casting his body into relief like a raised figure on a bowl, emanating power and muted emotion and hiding his face in shadow.

'You *want* me. That is quite different. Vincent offers me security and a good life with many interesting places to see, things to do; contentment.'

'And love? You haven't mentioned love.'

'Of course he loves me. He is devoted to me.'

'And you?' The dark shape was close, like a poised eagle or the giant roc that seized the unwary and flew off with them into the void.

'I . . . love him, too.'

'I love Roma and lots of other people, but I have no intention of spending my good life with them,' he said reasonably.

'That's different. I love people like that, too.'

'Vincent?'

'Don't be stupid. You know what I mean.' She tried to back away but he was there even though he seemed not to have moved an inch. 'He offers me everything a woman could want.'

'Security.' His voice was flat, as if he had said a bad word. 'Security and possessions.'

'Is that so bad, if I can't . . .'

'If you can't what?' The words came out sharp and loud.

'If I can't find what I need in my work,' she said feebly.

He took a fold of her dress. It glowed like a drying dragon-fly and as he dropped it, the fabric moulded back to her shape. 'You aren't greedy,' he said. 'You settle for work or security with someone you quite like.'

She smiled faintly. It was so close to the truth. 'I am not a first year nurse, all starry-eyed and ready for Romance with a capital R.'

'You were once.' He bent and touched the

corner of her mouth. 'It would be fun finding out if it is still there.' She drew in a sharp breath. 'Security. When did that concern you? You were meant to fly, not to sit on the ground and be afraid to move.'

'I've changed. We all change in time, even you.'

'So we grow up and like Chopin instead of bebop and good wine instead of warm beer in your terrible pubs.'

'It's better now after the American invasion, and you still like chocolate cake.' She touched the door handle and he seemed to draw away. 'I ought to ring the hotel and say I'm coming.'

'No need. I said that when you were ready to come, I'd put you in a taxi.' He felt the coffee-pot and shrugged. 'If you were staying, I'd make more, but it's up to you.'

She put a hand lightly over the burn, which began to itch under the dressing. 'It's irritating,' she said.

'What is? Vincent and this evening, the fact that you want more coffee, or your burn?'

'Everything. I don't know what I want any more.'

'I've known what I want for a very long time.'

'I can't have everything I want,' she said sadly. 'If I once gave in and took something, it might never be complete and I'd rather live with someone who would never change, never give me cause to worry, than to wonder if I had a complete man and his love.'

She hung her head and her hair softly hid her eyes. Orson brushed it back from her face. 'You know something? Once upon a time I was told a load of lies about the woman I loved, and I fell for it. If I hadn't been so hot for you, I could have laughed it off and even accepted it if it was true, but being Heavy Harry, I couldn't take it. And you were the same. We have a lot to thank Sister March for, Kaye. It was only a while ago that I found out how that dame's mind works, like a mole in dirt, burrowing and sending up piles of filth. I came back and saw you with that guy at the concert and thought maybe some of it was true, but inside I couldn't believe you'd ever let him take you, kiss you, love you.'

His hands twined in her hair and her face had to look up at him. He kissed her cheek and brushed her hair with his lips.

'I know you heard about me, too. And I knew you were too proud to ask just as I was. Then I saw glimpses of the real Kaye when you bent over a child, spoke to a porter about his wife, cared for little boys with ugly ears.'

A sob escaped her and tears formed on the edges of her long eyelashes. If it could be true, even for a while, then she must give up all her carefully built up barriers and be as vulnerable as a crab without a shell. She saw his face through a haze and knew his suffering. Her face rested on his chest and he held her close.

'I was never unfaithful,' she said at last.

'Hush, baby, I know. And even when I showed I liked women, you were the one I wanted for keeps. I played around on the surface, just for the hell of it. Life was good and I like to be liked, but it never went deep. You have to believe it.'

He pulled her after him into a deep armchair and she snuggled close against his side. He laughed softly.

'Hello, chair. It's the same one, with room for two.' He kissed her deeply and with controlled passion and his hands did wonderful things to her awareness. It was madness, she told herself, but she was past caring if tomorrow he looked at another girl.

'Well, you have a choice, Sister Kaye.'

'I have? I thought you were taking away my options.'

'You either ask me nicely to get you a taxi—and remember, the request has to come from you—or you swear that you have finished with business dinners and will come with me across continents and see marvellous sunsets.'

'All that, tonight?' She was strangely at peace.

'Choose,' he said.

'It's too late for a taxi, and I have a bad arm.'

'Quite right, but you don't think you get away with that. What about the other decision?'

'I'll think about it.' Kaye still needed time to put behind her the chaos caused by this one man who offered no safe place, but she knew that all the safety she wanted was in the circle of his arms.

'Marry me tomorrow, and we can find an apartment close to the hospital until we finish here. Then, who knows? We can ride the rainbow and find what we want with each other.'

'Marry you? You once said you weren't the marrying kind.' Joy welled up on a wave of sudden comprehension and she kissed him almost shyly. 'I'll marry you and live in a mud hut if that's what you want,' she said.

'Fine. Then I haven't wasted good money.'

'What do you mean?'

'I have one of your special licences signed by some great man. We can get married on Saturday.'

'You knew all along that I'd say yes. You . . . you . . . Oh, darling where have you been? I've missed you so.' He cradled her gently, murmuring soft words.

'You can't just take a woman to get married without rings and things. There will be lots to do.' She struggled up. 'I'll make more coffee.'

He watched her smooth down her dress and try to tidy her hair and he laughed. She looked at the door and then at him and saw the small box in his hand with the twin rings nesting there.

'Come here,' he said, 'I've got a cold spot this side.'

Mills & Boon

4 Doctor Nurse Romances
FREE

Coping with the daily tragedies and ordeals of a busy hospital, and sharing the satisfaction of a difficult job well done, people find themselves unexpectedly drawn together. Mills & Boon Doctor Nurse Romances capture perfectly the excitement, the intrigue and the emotions of modern medicine, that so often lead to overwhelming and blissful love. By becoming a regular reader of Mills & Boon Doctor Nurse Romances you can enjoy SIX superb new titles every two months plus a whole range of special benefits: your very own personal membership card, a free newsletter packed with recipes, competitions, bargain book offers, plus big cash savings.

**AND an Introductory FREE GIFT for YOU.
Turn over the page for details.**

Fill in and send this coupon back today and we'll send you
4 Introductory
Doctor Nurse Romances yours to keep
FREE

At the same time we will reserve a subscription to Mills & Boon Doctor Nurse Romances for you. Every two months you will receive the latest 6 new titles, delivered direct to your door. You don't pay extra for delivery. Postage and packing is always completely Free. There is no obligation or commitment – you receive books only for as long as you want to.

It's easy! Fill in the coupon below and return it to
MILLS & BOON READER SERVICE, FREEPOST, P.O. BOX 236, CROYDON, SURREY CR9 9EL.

Please note: **READERS IN SOUTH AFRICA write to Mills & Boon Ltd., Postbag X3010, Randburg 2125, S. Africa.**

- - - - - - - - - - - - - - - -

FREE BOOKS CERTIFICATE

To: Mills & Boon Reader Service, FREEPOST, P.O. Box 236, Croydon, Surrey CR9 9EL.

Please send me, free and without obligation, four Dr. Nurse Romances, and reserve a Reader Service Subscription for me. If I decide to subscribe I shall receive, following my free parcel of books, six new Dr. Nurse Romances every two months for £6.00*, post and packing free. If I decide not to subscribe, I shall write to you within 10 days. The free books are mine to keep in any case. I understand that I may cancel my subscription at any time simply by writing to you. I am over 18 years of age.

Please write in BLOCK CAPITALS.

Name _____

Address _____

_____

_____ Postcode _____

SEND NO MONEY — TAKE NO RISKS

EP15